Date of a Lifetime

Lynne Marshall

D1012084

HARLEQUIN

SPECIAL
EDITION

Recycling programs
for this product may
not exist in your area.

ISBN-13: 978-1-335-89450-2

Date of a Lifetime

Harlequin Enterprises ULC
22 Adelaide St. West, 40th Floor
Toronto, Ontario M5H 4E3, Canada
www.Harlequin.com

Printed in U.S.A.

Lynne Marshall used to worry she had a serious problem with daydreaming, and then she discovered she was supposed to write those stories down! A late bloomer, she came to fiction writing after her children were nearly grown. Now she battles the empty nest by writing romantic stories about life, love and happy endings. She's a proud mother and grandmother who loves babies, dogs, books, music and traveling.

Books by Lynne Marshall

Harlequin Special Edition

The Taylor Triplets

Cooking Up Romance

The Delaneys of Sandpiper Beach

Forever a Father
Soldier, Handyman, Family Man
Reunited with the Sheriff

Her Perfect Proposal
A Doctor for Keeps
The Medic's Homecoming
Courting His Favorite Nurse

Visit the Author Profile page
at Harlequin.com for more titles.

To my Date of a Lifetime, sweet William.
Thirty-eight years and counting...
Best decision I ever made.

Chapter One

Eva DeLongpre opened her computer for some precious time to work while her eleven-month-old son, Noah, took his morning nap. The small wood-floored office in her Santa Barbara home overlooked the grassy backyard, surrounded by trees that had survived last year's fires. The woodsy scent of the California bay laurel permeated the air thanks to the open window. She loved her yard and everything about the home she'd managed to purchase with her nana's help last year. Living in the lap of luxury, Eva would forever be grateful for that trust fund.

Following in her mother's footsteps by juggling a job and an adopted child had proved to be more complicated than she'd expected. Over the past year she'd learned how difficult it was, and almost cut her often-missing-in-action mother some slack because of it. Almost. Truth was, if it hadn't been for Nana, Eva would have been even lonelier as an only child. Nana had infused the extra love Eva longed for into her life while growing up. Determined not to let a job overtake home life with her child, like her mother had, Eva had vowed, on the day the adoption became official, to work out of the home and to spend as much time as possible with Noah.

Opening the Dreams Come True website email, she found a new batch of messages from senior citizens. Since her move, she'd changed from the Los Angeles youth division to the County of Santa Barbara over-sixty crowd at the nonprofit organization. As she read through the latest requests, one immediately grabbed her attention.

> *My name is Savannah Schuster. I'm eighty-four and have recently been diagnosed with early dementia. I'm an old maid—that's what we called it in my generation—aka a spinster.*

"These days we say single, Ms. Schuster," Eva spoke to the computer. "Like me."

> *I'm a retired secretary, have never been married and haven't had a boyfriend or a date in a long, long time.*

Your company claims to make dreams come true, and my dream is to have a date with a handsome man just once in my life. I have someone in mind, not anyone famous or out of reach, but won't say who unless I get a response from you.

The main thing is, I'd like to have this dream date while I can still remember it.

Time is running out! Can you help me?
Sincerest thanks,
Savannah

In the past, Eva would've conferred with coworkers before granting the most unusual wishes. However, these days the first person she consulted for just about everything was her newfound twin sister, Lacy.

"You won't believe this," Eva said as soon as Lacy answered her cell phone.

Having been separated at birth and unaware of it for over thirty years, then finding each other through a series of random encounters when it would be more likely to get hit by lightning, they made it a point to be there for each other. Lacy always took Eva's calls, and vice versa.

"I'm in the middle of making a dozen wraps to go. Can I call you right back?"

"Of course!"

"Give me fifteen. Talk soon."

Lacy owned and operated a food truck, and since

that was her livelihood, the demand for business had to come first. Eva completely understood.

If it hadn't been for that bright pink food truck and, more important, the owner operator with copper-red hair and blue eyes looking exactly like Eva and catching a coworker's eye, Eva may never have met her twin. Whether it was accidental or meant to be, Eva would be forever grateful they'd found each other. If only it could've happened sooner.

Her friends had called the discovery an amazing coincidence, but Eva and Lacy agreed: their finding each other after thirty-one years had to be fate. They'd shared a womb for nearly nine months and both had gone through life feeling something was missing. Living incomplete to a deeper degree than either could imagine, they'd both yearned for something they couldn't name. Until they'd come face-to-face that day one month ago at Zack Gardner's construction site.

While waiting for Lacy's return call, Eva reread Ms. Schuster's email and became curious about who the "date" she had in mind might be. Eva replied to the email, not confirming the wish would be granted but asking for more information. After all, Savannah had said she'd only disclose who the person was if she got a reply. Nothing more.

It also gave her time to reconsider privacy issues regarding sharing with her sister. She'd never had to think of that before and it was one more thing that made her smile these days.

Eva received a reply within a couple of minutes, leaving her to believe the eighty-four-year-old was either glued to her home computer or had a cell phone and knew how to use it! Never underestimate the seniors, she'd come to realize over the past six months in her position. Even if they used outdated and sometimes politically incorrect expressions. "Spinster" and "old maid" came quickly to mind.

I've always dreamed of having a date with a handsome politician since the Jack Kennedy days back in the early 1960s. These days I've been following a local and very handsome politician from my hometown. Mayor Joe Aguirre of Little River Valley.

The fact she wrote texts in complete sentences without a single abbreviation confirmed she was a senior citizen. Why a politician? Eva could hardly stomach politics, let alone politicians. But this wasn't her wish, it was Savannah's. And budgetwise, a dinner tab in a local restaurant could be a more doable proposition. The charity's mission statement promised to bring joy and beauty into the lives of those facing the challenges of life threatening and/or chronic disease in the last stage of life. Joy and beauty, as with most things in life, were in the eye of the beholder, Eva reminded herself.

Her cell rang and Lacy's bright, familiar face

popped up, which still rattled her because of the resemblance. "Hey! Can I run something by you?"

"Of course."

"Theoretically..." Eva paraphrased the email
without giving away her potential client's identifi-
cation.

Lacy's laugh always got Eva going, and they spent
a few moments enjoying their chuckles about one
of the oddest requests she'd had since joining the
nonprofit.

"Here this person is with an uncertain future, and
all she wants is a date."

"She's sincere," Lacy added. "Kind of tugs at my
heart."

"I know. That's why I love my job so much. I get
to help people do what they could never arrange on
their own. Especially while dealing with illness or
insecure finances."

"You should do it!" Lacy said without hesitation.
"We know him and he's a good guy." Since Lacy
had lived all her life in Little River Valley fifteen
miles inland from Santa Barbara—Eva's most recent
hometown—she took this as a strong endorsement.

She leaned back in the dark oakwood swivel chair
at her sturdy desk, glancing out the window as she
thought briefly.

"Then I'll get the paperwork going on this wish
request and email her back." Though Eva had a full-
body cringe over the thought of spending time with

a politician, there was no way she would leave a newly diagnosed dementia patient on her own. Savannah deserved to have her date with a handsome man while she could still remember and enjoy it. Wasn't that all she'd asked? Also, a dream date would be an inexpensive wish. Win-win! And all Lacy's talk about this Joe being a great guy, and apparently being easy on the eyes, had piqued her interest.

She googled Mayor Joe Aguirre of Little River Valley and clicked on images. Yowza! Savannah had great taste. The stylish black hair, close-cropped on the sides and longish on top, complete with a side part, and the man's penetrating eyes beneath those dark brows sent a chill through her chest. Not to mention the classic Roman nose and sensual mouth. He looked sexy, *er* professional, in a suit, too. Maybe she could forget her aversion to all things politics for one night. For the sake of Savannah.

"Are you coming for dinner tonight?" Lacy asked.

"Wouldn't miss it!"

After a shy start, they'd shared a meal or coffee or at least a long phone conversation every single day since finding each other. Today would be no different. When Lacy cooked, Eva pigged out! Over the last month, after figuring out some personality differences, their friendship had grown by leaps and bounds. Finally, she had the sister she'd always longed for, right down to Lacy insisting Eva was a control freak, and Eva encouraging Lacy to step up her business game. Often, they'd had to agree to disagree and move on.

With a smile on her face, Eva went back to her computer, took another peep at the gorgeous mayor and moved on to the business side of her job. The paperwork. She'd made a name for herself making dreams come true for the last five years, establishing a charitable organization with some of Nana's trust fund money. She loved running a nonprofit. Didn't even mind all the fund-raising. How could Eva refuse her client's wish when she prided herself on making the most unusual wishes come true, and especially since this would be the one-hundredth wish Eva had granted in her short career. A milestone.

Last year, leaving the larger, more general side of the Los Angeles–based nonprofit in good hands, Eva created the senior citizens division in Santa Barbara after moving there. She'd wanted to honor her grandmother and this seemed the perfect way. Getting away from LA had helped her heal emotionally, too. She'd become too attached to one of her young Dreams Come True clients, and it had nearly broken Eva's heart. The relationship had certainly changed her life. The teenage mother had found out midway through her pregnancy that she had cancer, and her one wish, being that she'd lived all her short life in foster care, was for her baby to have a home. A real home.

As an adopted child herself, Eva had made the

decision without batting an eye, though until that moment she'd never planned on having a child while being single. Life could pitch screwballs that way, like finding her twin out of the blue!

She and Yolanda, Noah's mother, had bonded deeply and stayed in touch until a few months after the delivery, when the young woman succumbed to the cancer. But Yolanda had died knowing her healthy baby boy was in a loving home and that he'd never want for anything with Eva as his mother. If anyone had deserved peace of mind in her short life, it was Yolanda, and she had finally gotten hers.

Best decision Eva had ever made, though her life had changed drastically after taking on a child as a single parent. But all for the better.

Noah's lusty cry through the baby monitor alerted Eva. Nap time was over.

She tidied the few papers on her desk, pushed the chair in, padded across the hand-scraped wood floor and closed the door securely behind her. The office was the one place Noah didn't have free rein in the house.

They all sat around Zack Gardner's kitchen table best suited for two, three tops. Eva squeezed in beside Emma, Zack's ten-year-old daughter, like she always did whenever she dined with Lacy at her fiancé's house. After the initial "getting to know you" phase, she'd quickly become one of the extended family. What a difference one month could make.

"We'll do dinner the usual buffet style," Lacy said, addressing the problem from the oven, setting out the bubbling hot casserole beside a huge salad bowl along with fresh bread on the opposite counter. "Okay, line up. Emma, honey, why don't you start."

Emma, the aspiring junior chef, jumped at the chance, sniffing the air as if the finest cuisine had just been served. Eva had quickly learned her twin sister's curried chicken and broccoli dish could easily qualify for such a title—fine cuisine—and her mouth watered as she waited her turn. Lacy had also been teaching the girl the basics of cooking since meeting Zack a few months ago, and Emma had taught Lacy how to crochet in return. Something about that story always squeezed Eva's heart.

Noah sat in his portable high chair, kicking his feet, hands twisting and turning in anticipation of his turn. His dinner was not nearly as aromatic as the casserole, but healthily prepared by Eva with fresh-steamed and mashed broccoli and pulverized roasted chicken set aside by Lacy as she put the casserole together. Eleven-month-old Noah couldn't be trusted with bread since he would keep shoving it in until he gagged, so Eva served him cooked whole and ancient grains from her stash at home instead.

"We could branch out to the dining room table,

you know," tall, blond Zack said, last in line, having insisted Lacy go before him.

"I know, but it's cozier in here—less formal, right, Emma?" Lacy said with a wink.

"Right."

Eva loved how Lacy had found her way into their lives and how this table meant only for father and daughter, now managed to seat more. With just enough room for four plates and a glass each, they crowded around the table, elbows nearly touching, and Noah sitting a bit back between Emma and Eva as they began the meal.

"Lacy tells me you have a special request to grant."

"You mean the big date?" Eva lifted her gaze from the delicious food to her future brother-in-law, handsome and totally in love with her sister. "Yeah," she laughed lightly. "This sweet lady wants a date with a hot guy who happens to be your mayor."

"That's so cute," Lacy said. "Isn't that cute?" she looked to Emma for affirmation, who gladly made a huge nod. The girl clearly adored Lacy.

"We can arrange that, you know," Zack continued. "I've dealt extensively with Joe Aguirre on the senior housing project. He's a good guy. Never thought of him as 'hot,' though."

Eva smirked. "Not the usual slick what's-in-it-for-me politician-type?" She couldn't help her bias; she'd studied the news enough to figure out the trend.

"Not at all. He's lived here all his life and only wants what's best for us. He's the right guy for the job and we'd like to keep him in office. This 'date' might help."

"He's been getting a tough time from his opponent," Lacy added. "Because he vetoed a fast-food chain from building two drive-throughs. She claims our seniors need cheap places to eat to help stretch their fixed incomes."

Eva screwed up her face. "Fast food is the last thing they need."

"I know, right? They need healthy, nutritious meals, not that stuff loaded with salt and fat, begging for strokes," Lacy finished Eva's thought for her, as they often did since discovering each other. That part still amazed and sometimes creeped Eva out.

"I can call Joe tonight if you'd like."

"Thanks, Zack." Eva picked up a roll, broke it in half and buttered it as she spoke. "But I want to think this through a little more before I officially grant the woman's wish."

"Okay, but just keep in mind he could use a boost to his likability ratings, because his opponent has really been bad-mouthing him to the seniors around here. And the guy doesn't blow his own horn enough, in my opinion. Too humble, I guess. A date with a sweet senior could change more than a few minds."

Eva took a quick bite of dinner in between feeding Noah. Too humble? What a refreshing thought where politicians were concerned. "Sounds like you really support this guy."

"We do," Zack and Lacy said in unison.

"I'll get in touch as soon as I make up my mind, okay?" Noah was preoccupied with trying to pick up a tiny piece of farro from his tray with pincher-like precision, which gave Eva the chance to take another bite of delicious casserole and a couple chugs of water.

"Of course," Zack said before shoveling a forkful of chicken and broccoli dripping with mushrooms and cheddar cheese into his mouth.

"Speaking of getting in touch," Lacy piped up, "have you heard back from your mom yet?"

Eva shook her head, her mouth full. Her mother, rather than sticking around to be a grandmother when Eva adopted Noah, had embarked on a yearlong around-the-world cruise. Although Bridget's timing was unintentional, Eva had to concede, since she had already signed up for the cruise before Eva announced the adoption. Still, becoming a mom for the first time without experienced backup had been daunting.

The internet was spotty in most of the ports on the cruise, and Eva had lost track of where her nearly seventy-year-old mother currently was. "It's kind of like playing Where in the World Is Bridget De-Longpre."

That elicited a laugh out of Lacy, who always got her meager attempts at jokes. Carmen Sandiego. Bridget DeLongpre. Yeah, you had to be there in the 1990s. And one of the things Eva and Lacy had discovered about each other—they'd both been huge *Where in the World Is Carmen Sandiego* nerds. Which helped with the geography questions on *Jeopardy!* Something else they'd both admitted to being hooked on.

"I've tried to skype her, but she hasn't been available. I'll send another email and let her know you and I have more than a few questions to ask."

Just before Eva and Lacy officially met, Lacy had discovered in the attic some mysterious paperwork disclosing that her mother had adopted her a month after birth. Her father, who Lacy looked the spitting image of, hadn't had to do the same, and all Lacy wanted to know for now was if her father was her true birth father. Her hunch was, *absolutely.* The fact he'd died last year made it impossible to ask or to check out their DNA for a match. Of course, the DNA test was the first thing Eva and Lacy had done after they'd met, and as they'd guessed they were indeed identical twins.

They had so many questions about why the twins had been allowed to be separated at birth, and Bridget was either honestly inaccessible or running away from sharing the answer. Separating sisters? What a horrible idea! If any two people were owed the truth, it was Lacy and Eva.

Lacy gathered Emma's empty plate and stacked on her own dish. "Please keep trying. Have you had any luck finding any paperwork on *your* adoption?"

"With work and caring for Noah, honestly, I haven't had much time to snoop around my mom's place. Plus, it's over an hour's drive to Los Angeles." Eva ate the last bite and handed off her plate to Lacy. "Besides, it would feel a bit nefarious without getting her permission."

"I understand." Lacy took a sip of water before piling Eva's plate on top of the others and avoided making eye contact.

"All I know is it was a closed adoption." Which didn't bode well for getting to the bottom of their story without the help of Eva's adoptive mother.

Noah let out a squeal and upturned his empty bowl, obviously ready for more food, and in a group effort, everyone at the table jumped to meet one aspect of his needs. Zack refilled his sippy cup with water, Emma offered him one of her broccoli florets while he impatiently waited, Eva wiped up the mess on his high chair tray and Lacy made quick work of dishing out more pulverized cooked chicken.

Happy baby, happy life.

Joe Aguirre hardly had time to run Little River Valley and maintain his law practice, let alone raise funds and run for reelection against an aggressive opponent who wasn't above pulling dirty tricks. Like the fast-food shenanigans.

Sitting, Joe shuffled through a stack of papers on his messy desk, hoping to find the schedule his best friend and campaign manager, Mike Machado, had copied and personally handed him earlier in the afternoon. All work and no play had made him disorganized.

He shoved the ergonomically adjusted chair back from his functional, no-frills metal-and-glass desk and put his hands behind his head. All Joe was doing was honoring the town charter, written long before he'd been born, which declared no chain stores were allowed within the city limits. The townspeople had been perfectly happy with their own unique department store and numerous other small businesses, independent restaurants, cafés and diners all these years. Why change now?

Suddenly, with the campaign heating up, his opponent had begun to insist the seniors needed cheap, fast food. Change the Charter had become her slogan. Talk about convenient. He went back to searching for the misplaced schedule. "Where is it," he grumbled, ready to push everything off his table to find it if necessary.

He was wise enough to know this made-up problem by his opponent was in response to his attempt to balance the town budget. The exercise involved tightening a few bloated belts and cutting down al-

locations for some local government-funded businesses, one of which was owned by his opponent.
His decision to allow the building of a hundred
small homes for citizens sixty and over, instead of
letting the mega fast-food company have its way
with expanding wherever it pleased, had also irri-
tated a handful of local investors. People, he'd come
to find out, who'd moved to Little River Valley *after*
making their millions. People who had zero alle-
giance to his hometown and what it stood for. He'd
put his foot down, and fast, and now the backlash
was an opponent, probably backed by them, who
suddenly couldn't live without the Golden Arches
in her backyard.

Change the Charter over my dead body.

His cell phone rang and he grabbed it, putting it
immediately to speaker. "Aguirre."

"Joe!"

Speak of the devil. It was his best friend, the
last person he wanted to talk to tonight. "*Que pasa*,
Miguel?"

"Have you seen the latest poll?"

Could he please stop with the continuous updates
on the uphill battle? Yes, Joe had seen that poll, thank
you very much, and he didn't want to be reminded
about Louella Barnstable's tightening of his lead.

"We need some good PR and fast. Got any ideas?"

"Honestly?" Joe tossed his pen on the mounting

pile of papers on his desk. "If running on my good record isn't enough, I don't have a clue."

"That's your problem, you're too pragmatic. You need to show more personality, flash that handsome smile more often."

"Not my style and you know it."

"If Louella keeps gaining on you, you're going to have to come up with something, so you better start thinking now."

He dug thumbs in his closed eyes and squinted tight. "Okay, I'll smile more. Kiss more babies."

"That's right. Get seen. Shake hands."

He knew the drill but dreaded it. Not that he didn't like or care about people. Why else would he be running for a second term as mayor? But his law practice was suffering from inattention. He hadn't been able to take on a new client in months, and truth was, since he didn't intend to be mayor for life, it worried him. That and the fact that *man did not live from small-town mayoral salary alone.* "I promise to be on Main Street walking the boulevard first thing tomorrow morning."

"And eat breakfast at Donna Lee's."

"Good idea." The quintessential small-town greasy spoon diner. "I'll let people know there are plenty of places to get good inexpensive meals in town. Served on plates, not in paper bags. Don't they have an early bird special? We don't need fast food. Not in Little River Valley."

"That's the spirit. Be sure to let the *Little River Valley Voice* know you'll be there, too."

"Isn't that your job?"

"Okay, *bueno*. Meantime, I'll keep my eye out for any and all PR opportunities."

Joe rubbed his face with a hand. This was the part he hated about running for public office. He couldn't be spontaneous. Had to have his campaign manager tip off the newspaper whenever he went out, to make sure he was seen and so the story got covered. Kind of like the debate about sound and the tree falling in the forest. If Joe wasn't seen out and about in Little River Valley, did he exist?

Yes, he grumbled internally. Because he was always working. For the citizens of Little River Valley. "Great. Sounds good. *Buenos noches*, Miguel."

"It's Mike to you, *Jose*."

Ending the call with the friendly reminder that Jose and Miguel had been childhood friends helped Joe smile. First day of elementary school, the six-year-old boys had been thrown together in an English only, total immersion setting. Joe's parents only knew enough English to get along on the job and spoke *solamente* Spanish at home. Joe had only picked up a few English phrases from watching TV. Both boys had been thankful they didn't have to go through the trauma alone and had bonded immediately. Friends for life. They'd both come a long way from the Ventura County barrio; and their parents, who'd spent most of their lives breaking their backs on the local farmlands to help them get out, had a lot to be proud of.

Chapter Two

Donna Lee's was a small but always busy breakfast-and-lunch diner in the heart of the city, and Joe showed up bright and early. A table had been reserved for him, by Mike, of course. The server led him there. Though Joe would've been happier to sit at the counter with the early-morning work crowd drinking coffee and chowing down his eggs. They were the folks he felt the most comfortable with, the ones he represented, people on their way to jobs that kept the city alive. The everyday employees and small business employers. The last thing he needed was a reserved booth separating him from them.

"Thank you," he said to the middle-aged woman,

Mandy, as he took a seat in the booth meant for four, feeling a little foolish. She wore a super short silver haircut and dangly blue-beaded earrings, most likely made by her. They'd talked about her love of crafts on other occasions. Today the place was bustling and there was hardly time for pleasantries, let alone a real conversation. Dressed in the restaurant uniform, a dark blue polo shirt with the diner logo above the pocket, she left the menu and promised coffee was on the way. Leave Full or Blame Yourself, the logo said in large letters across the back of her shirt.

The booth was by the front window, so he gazed outside and watched the early-morning activity on Main Street. It made him smile. Joe quietly shook his head, sure as ever Mike had meticulously arranged where he should sit for the best photo op this morning. Taking care of every detail, as Mike always did as the campaign manager. Limelight was the guy's middle name.

The place had been remodeled a few years back, and all the old pink Formica tabletops and black-and-white tiled floors were replaced with wood. The tables were highly varnished, and the floor planks were pre-distressed, giving the place a rustic and comfortable appeal. He liked it, and also noticed the new cushion on the upholstered booth seat was already worn down from constant use.

Thinking of Mike and his implicit instructions, Joe looked around the nearly full-to-capacity diner, nodding and smiling pleasantly at anyone looking his way.

As promised, Mandy came back and filled his coffee cup. He'd spent so much time looking around the packed diner and out the window that he'd forgotten to look at the menu she handed him. Then, midpour, his old friend showed up.

"Mike, what a surprise," he said, droll as could be, knowing Mike understood.

"Couldn't let my best friend eat alone," Mike said, waving over the photographer from the *Little River Valley Voice* and asking the server to stick around for an opportunity shot. She didn't look comfortable with the instruction.

Joe cringed inside. "You don't have to, Mandy."

"Not crazy about pictures, but for you, Joe, I will. I mean Mayor Aguirre."

"Just Joe. And thanks." He wasn't crazy about opportunity shots, either, but went along with it for the sake of his campaign, and his pal. As always, he had to think of the bigger goal.

Once that was over, she blushed with the honor of getting her picture in the paper, then waited patiently while they quickly read the menu before taking their orders.

"Ah." After a slurp of his black coffee, Mike said, "So I got an interesting message this morning."

"And does this message involve me?" Joe also

took a sip and had to admit the diner made great coffee.

Mike gave his signature full-toothed grin, thick cheeks accentuating his dimples. "These days *everything* involves you. You, my friend, *light up my life*."

"Stop with the bull—"

"Okay," Mike broke in before Joe could be heard swearing in public. "Ever hear of Dreams Come True?"

"Is it a song?"

Mike gave a pointed and mocking stare.

Okay. "Can't say I have."

"Well, it's a nonprofit that grants wishes to people. Like the Make-A-Wish Foundation, except this one is for senior citizens."

"Okay." Joe waited patiently for the full explanation.

Mike took another drink of coffee, building suspense as only he could, the steam circling his long nose. "Apparently a senior citizen has made a wish involving you."

"Me?" Joe scrunched up his face just as the newspaper photographer flashed another shot. So much for the staged photo. In his gut, Joe suspected this one, the caught-off-guard picture with his mouth open, would run in its place. Though that could be one way to figure out if the city rag supported him or *her*. As yet, they hadn't come out with a statement. "What did they wish for?"

"Got to call the woman back to find out, but it must involve you, right?" Mike jumped up and headed outside, evidently deciding there was no time like the present to find out.

Joe looked at his watch. 8:05 a.m. He doubted anyone would take the call at this hour. His breakfast got delivered, and rather than wait for Mike, he dug in, letting Mandy know immediately how great the Denver omelet was, and asking her to tell the chef, as she refilled both the coffee cups. She smiled extra sweetly at him, and thankfully, the photographer from the booth across the way took another picture. At least this one wasn't staged.

By the time Mike returned, Joe was nearly done with his breakfast while Mike's sunny-side-up eggs had gotten cold.

"Great news," Mike said, not caring about the state of his eggs and digging a piece of toast into the first yolk. "You, sir," he continued dipping the bread, yellow goo dripping off the sourdough, "are on the bucket list of a sweet eighty-four-year-old named Savannah Schuster." Only then did he shove half the toast in his mouth and chew, letting his supposedly earth-shattering news sink in.

Mike was ever the one for dramatic effect. Joe grinned inwardly but kept a serious expression while motioning for Mike to dab drippage from the corner of his mouth with a napkin and waiting for the rest of the story.

Mike explained every detail that the woman named Evangelina DeLongpre from Dreams Come True had described over the phone. Joe sat silent, wondering what this had to do with the campaign.

"Don't you see? This is exactly what you need." Mike leaned in and lowered his voice. "That shot in the arm you so desperately need right now. A senior citizen wants a date with you. It's priceless."

"And this will help how?"

"An adoring senior citizen from our very own town believes in you and longs to spend an evening with *you*. Did I mention she has early dementia and time is of the essence?"

"Do you seriously think this is a good idea?"

In short order, Mike had managed to demolish his breakfast. "The best idea," he said, mouth covered by the napkin. He pulled his usual pregnant pause by taking a last quaff of his coffee. "This will show your compassionate side. I say 'show,' which is really important. It's putting action to your words. We know you care about senior citizens. I tell people, you tell people, but this will *show* you in action. Imagine. You taking this little old lady out for an evening she'll never forget." He realized his error in exaggeration quickly. "I mean, it will be the biggest night of her life since turning eighty, and you can't take that away from her, even when her memory goes. Got it?"

Joe inhaled. "Let me think about this. It feels a

little too much like a stunt. I don't want to come off that way."

"It's only a stunt if we orchestrate it."

Joe tilted his head, eyes narrowing, weighing the difference.

Mike's thick brows lifted. "Okay, think about it, but just until the end of the day. It's important that we act soon. And as your campaign manager, I'm advising you to do this."

"I'll let you know this afternoon," Joe said, standing and leaving a big tip before taking the bill to the cash register to pay. As he turned to leave the diner, one last camera flash blinded him before he stepped out into the full-on sun.

Later in the day, after speaking at the local high school PTA, Joe planned to get some personal work done. No sooner had he sat down at his desk than he got a call.

"Mayor Aguirre, I'm so glad I caught you in your office," Eva DeLongpre said after introducing herself.

Lately his normal law office had become a madhouse because it doubled as campaign headquarters. It wasn't ethical to use the mayor's office for reelection purposes, which was probably why she'd called him here and not there. Normally, several of the locals, mostly high schoolers and town moms, plus a few senior citizens, volunteered to take his calls so he could attempt to get personal work done. Apparently no one had been scheduled today.

He crinkled his nose, hoping he hadn't made a mistake answering the phone for his missing volunteer. Uh. "I like to help out when I can," he said.

"I was hoping by now Mr. Machado has spoken to you about the request from Dreams Come True?"

Ah, the date! He pinched the bridge of his nose. "As a matter of fact, he has, and I think it's a great idea." Keep it humble. "Though I can't imagine why Ms. Schuster picked me."

"You remind her of Jack Kennedy."

The comment stopped him. The great President Kennedy? "Really?" In what way? He suddenly had a hundred questions but no time.

"Yes. You'd make Savannah a very happy woman if you'd agree to the date. She's been newly diagnosed with dementia, as you might know, and with the anxiety about her future and all, well, let's just say you'd be a wonderful distraction for her. One evening. One memorable meal she can hold on to until…"

"Until it's gone. I understand."

"She's a good lesson on living in the moment, and right this moment, she's asking for you."

"Because George Clooney is busy, I take it."

Her lilting laugh surprised him. He liked it.

"On the contrary, you were her first and only choice."

"Well, then." His father had always taught him, when speaking to people, to not talk about himself, but to turn the conversation around to the other person. "And how did you get involved in granting wishes?" Man, he sounded like a politician.

There went that inviting laugh again. "Professional wish-granter. I should add that to my business card." She paused. "I guess you could say I've always wanted to give back to my community." Then she sighed. "Truth is, I've had it pretty good all my life and wasn't sure I deserved it."

She sounded sincere enough with the honest answer. "That's commendable. And your background is?"

"Business major in college. A minor in psychology. A nonprofit seemed a good fit."

"Yes, I'd say so, too." His BS-ometer had yet to register. There was a genuine quality to her conversation, but he still wasn't ready to commit. "Well, give me a little more time to look over my calendar, would you please, Ms. DeLongpre."

"Of course, and please call me Eva."

"Okay, Eva, I promise to get back to you before the end of the day."

They said their goodbyes, and something about her soft-spoken voice lingered in his head. Something nice had just gone on, and it had been a long time since he'd "noticed" such things. He almost smiled, but his long-term companion of mistrust in all things female beat him to the moment. Instead, he hitched one side of his mouth. "Hmm. I wonder what her real angle is?"

Before making his decision about whether to agree—or not—to what he sensed could be perceived as a publicity stunt, he went online.

First he went to the Dreams Come True website and read their mission statement. The nonprofit appeared to be serving a noble cause for senior citizens, no doubt about that, with many folks having had significant requests met. Savannah's wish seemed trivial in comparison, except for the fact she knew she had dementia and would lose her memory in due course. If it meant that much to her to have dinner with Joe, why shouldn't he do it?

Then Joe clicked on the staff and singled out Evangelina DeLongpre. Wow. She looked a lot like Lacy Winters, Zack Gardner's fiancée. Maybe they were related? Though Eva's red hair was pulled back into some kind of knot. Her eyes, which were perfectly made up, were striking. They were blue like tinted crystals, almost unreal. It was obviously a touched-up professional headshot, and he wasn't going to get carried away by her beauty. In his experience, looks were *always* deceiving.

He read her biography. Just what he didn't need in his life, another spoiled rich girl. This one playing philanthropist. She'd hinted about her privilege on the phone, but it hadn't brushed him the wrong way then. Maybe because she sounded a little guilty about it?

No doubt he had a jaded view of that type of woman thanks to his past. Briefly he castigated himself for labeling Evangelina because of Victoria Harrington but ran with his thoughts anyway. Evangelina hit all the criteria for SRG, from her name to where she grew up—affluent Hancock Park, Los Angeles—to where she went to college—East Coast Ivy League, Dartmouth. Both prestigious and expensive. He knew the breed well.

He'd had his fill of such types in college, after falling in love with one. All he'd wanted was to please her, to make her happy. She'd liked the sex just fine, but remained aloof, no matter what he did or how hard he tried, he wasn't able to tear down her wall. Meanwhile, he'd confused love with worship, the worst possible combination with a woman like Victoria. Nothing he did was good enough. No achievement great enough. And she seemed to take pleasure in letting him know.

To this day he hated the fact he'd been helplessly in love with Victoria. After a long and messy breakup, she'd crushed him, leaving him thinking he simply wasn't good enough for her and never could be. Being honest, even today, he was still trying to prove to her, and anyone like her, that they were wrong. He didn't need money or status. He was worthy as he was. *Keep repeating until you believe it.*

"Money doesn't equal worth," he said quietly as he dug deeper into Evangelina DeLongpre's history. Her mother, Bridget DeLongpre, had been the real estate agent to the stars in Los Angeles in the 1990s and into the early 2000s and onward, only recently retiring. Eva was most likely a trust fund baby who probably never had to work a day in her life. Yet, unlike Victoria, who embraced her privilege with everything she had, Ms. DeLongpre had started a nonprofit. To help others. That was completely different than Victoria, who'd gone on to marry a neurosurgeon. From what he'd read in the Santa Barbara newspaper society section, the only charity Victoria dealt with was planning balls for the rich and famous. A tiny voice wondered if she even knew he was the mayor of Little River Valley.

Who needed the aggravating and humiliating reminder?

Old resentment got the better of him and he wanted to think the worst of Eva, simply because of Victoria. He needed to let it go and think reasonably. Prove he'd moved on, if not emotionally, at least professionally.

Eva DeLongpre had *chosen* to work. As much as he wanted to resent her, the fair play side of his brain wouldn't let him. But he'd certainly be on the lookout for any clues *if* he decided to go along with Savannah's wish.

He scrolled through the list of seniors that Dreams

Come True had helped. Each person had been given a wish they could never pull off on their own, and many of those wishes had been quite amazing and costly. Savannah came to mind with her simple and, if he wanted to be honest, sweet wish to spend the evening having dinner and drinks with a man she respected and felt—Joe begged to differ with the description—was handsome. He'd never think of himself that way.

Rugged, maybe.

That got him laughing at himself. Rugged. Seriously? "This is ridiculous," he said to the computer screen. So he shut down the website.

He wasn't in the rich girl league, for sure. He was nearly forty years old, barely making ends meet on the personal level, trying his best to rationalize spending his small retirement fund on the reelection campaign. Why did he do it again?

Because his constituents needed *him*, not that Louella Barnstable!

And here was one free and huge campaign booster falling right into his lap. He needed to put his personal objections aside. What was the harm? Besides, it was high time he forgot how he loathed spoiled rich girls. He could do that for one night in order to make a sweet little senior lady happy. Couldn't he?

He picked up his cell. "Call Mike," he instructed.

"Yo!" His best friend answered on the first ring.

"Okay, let's do it. How soon can you set up the dinner date?"

* * *

On Friday afternoon Eva tried on a third dress, this one black, with a boatneck, cap sleeves and a classic form-fit to midknee, and made a slow turn for Lacy. "Think simple string of pearls and black three-inch pointy pumps?"

"Nice, but if it were me, I'd go with the first one, the peacock blue that fits like…"

"A condom?" Eva blurted a quick laugh as Lacy blushed. They'd already figured out how their upbringing had made them different. Hometown vs slick city girl. "Not the message I want to send! Which is exactly why I'll wear this." Eva preferred to think she'd evolved to sophisticated.

"I get that the dinner is granting Ms. Schuster's wish, but…"

"Which is why I want to stay in the background. I'm nothing more than a facilitator." She reached behind and unzipped herself. "The only reason I'm going is because of Savannah's early dementia." She slipped out of the dress, her mind made up. "Never thought I'd be a chaperone for an eighty-four-year-old."

"I love your job!"

Eva put her knuckles on her waist. "I love *your* job!" At times like this, what she'd give to drive a bright pink food truck for one day, just to see how it felt. But then, of course, she'd also have to know how to cook.

Lacy stepped closer and hugged her sister, then they stood side by side and looked in the mirror. Eva in a skimpy slip, Lacy in jeans and a pale blue cotton top. Same height, only five pounds of disparity between Eva and Lacy, who had the rounder hips and slightly fuller breasts. They studied each other in the mirror for a few seconds.

"All those years I knew something was missing, and now here you are, my other half," Eva said, more content than she'd ever been in thirty-one years. That is, after she'd gotten over the shock of discovering she was a twin.

"And I'm the only person in the world who knows exactly how you feel about that."

Looking into her sister's face, Eva was granted the gift of knowing how she looked to other people when she smiled. Still, she bet Lacy's smile was brighter, less cautious. More beautiful. Because she loved her twin.

Stinging eyes were the price of times like these, the good kind of tears, yet Eva didn't think she'd ever get used to seeing her double.

"Okay." Lacy was the first to speak, wiping at her lashes. "Be yourself tonight. You can trust Joe. He's one of the good ones."

"I feel like you've told me that at least a dozen times."

"I'm just thinking it wouldn't hurt for you to find a man, someone like Joe, for instance, who also hasn't found the right person yet. Mainly because he's as busy as you are."

"I get it, I get it. But this is a professional event, nothing more."

"Maybe, maybe not." Lacy toed the plush rug. "When opportunity knocks…"

"He's a mayor of a small town taking the opportunity to shine for his constituents. Nothing more."

"And I'm just saying, maybe look beyond that because he's also a good man. Quality over fortune. That's my point." Tired of playing with the plastic blocks, Noah crawled over and Lacy picked him up.

Eva pulled on a loose mustard yellow sweatshirt. "Are you accusing me of being snooty?"

"Never. But most of us have no idea what it's like to grow up rich."

"Trust me—" Eva put a leg into her designer jeans, then the other "—it's not what it's cracked up to be."

Lacy gazed at Eva's overstocked closet to make an obvious point. "Mmm-hmm."

"Borrow anything you'd like, anytime." Eva used fingers to put her hair back in place in front of the closet door.

Lacy rolled her eyes and Eva caught her through the mirror. "I know, Ms. Cleavage, the dresses might be a little snug, but Zack would love it. In fact, borrow the peacock blue one! Knock the man over the head!"

Lacy's cheeks turned pink. "We're pretty darn great in that department without your help, thank you very much."

"You think I don't know that?" She turned to face Lacy. "All I have to do is see how he looks at you." Eva stared down her sister, wondering what having a relationship with a man like that might be like. Her experience in relationships had been mostly the kind nightmares were made of. "You're one lucky woman."

Lacy took the moment and savored it, all the while holding a squirmy Noah. Eva saw the light bulb go off. "Now we've got to find someone for you."

Eva shook her head, the thought of ever opening her heart again scaring the breath out of her lungs, sorry she'd brought up the subject of happy relation-ships. "Not a team effort. But thanks. I'll get by."

"I know it's hard with a baby and work, but I'll babysit whenever you want." Lacy glanced at Noah and pretended to pinch his healthy cheeks. "Right, sweetie? We love spending time together, huh."

"Like tonight."

"Yup."

"Except tonight is business only."

"Right. Is everything packed up for him?"

"Yes. And I can't thank you enough. It should be an early night. We've hired a limousine and a driver. You can expect me before ten."

"Okay. He'll be fast asleep in the portable bed

in our guest room. He could spend the night just as easily, you know."

Eva gave a dead stare.

"Okay. Just use your key and let yourself in."

"Will do."

"Good luck tonight!"

Eva's stomach fluttered remembering her reaction while talking to Mayor Joe Aguirre the other day. The man seemed genuinely nice. Why did tonight feel like such a big deal?

Eva rapped on door twenty-three in the peach-colored hall of the assisted-living facility, having the distinct impression this was what hotels were like in the 1950s. Except each apartment was individualized by the tenant. Some had fake plants out front, others, glass cases with memorabilia from their lives. One even had a round-back wicker chair to sit in, as though on a porch, and people sat in hallways all the time. Other doorways were less ornate. Savannah's had a large dog statue outside with a small flowering houseplant on the canine's flattened head.

Yipping and scratching came from the other side of the door. Some small creature obviously wanted to tear Eva apart.

"Nipsey. Quiet!" came from inside in a surprisingly strong voice.

Eva was glad she hadn't worn nylons, or they'd be about to get shredded by what sounded like an ankle biter. The door was opened by a white-haired woman, and a dog effortlessly leaped over the woman's foot, meant to guard the animal from getting out. "Hello, I'm Savannah," the woman managed to say as the dog barked louder, escaping into the hall. Eva stepped back.

"Nipsey, stop that!" Savannah said, as if the dog had never done such a thing before. Which Eva soundly doubted. Intent on sniffing everything below Eva's knees, Nipsey ignored its master.

Eva kept moving away from the ever-advancing dog. "Is your dog a biter?"

Savannah glanced at Eva as if she'd grown a second head. "No. Nipsey just gets excited." She bent down in a surprisingly limber fashion and scooped up the short-legged white-and-brown terrier. "Come in."

With trepidation, Eva did. The small apartment smelled of yesterday's cabbage or bell peppers and was decorated exactly as she would expect for a grandmother type. Sturdy dark tables, an overstuffed love seat with one matching chair and blue plaid upholstery that had seen better days. Marty Bell—or was it Thomas Kinkade?—cottage paintings framed in dark wood covered the walls. The dog continued to bark and had now added growling to the repertoire.

"So is *Nipsey* a boy or girl?"

Savannah let the dog down and it jumped around in a circle like a wind-up toy, as it showed off with the escalating barking. "A boy. A hyperactive and funny boy. Aren't you?" she said to the dog. "Sometimes he kills me." She focused back on Eva. "I named him after the comedian."

Absolutely nothing came to mind. Had there ever been a comedian named Nipsey?

"Kind of a play on words. Because he's a Jack *Russell* terrier. Get it?" Savannah waited for Eva to guess. The answer didn't come. "You know, *Nipsey Russell*," Savannah prodded.

Eva couldn't help the blank expression.

"Come on, the man used to open for Sergio Franchi in Vegas and was on *The Dean Martin Show* all the time. You never heard of Nipsey Russell?" Savannah eyed Eva suspiciously as though they no longer inhabited the same planet. Even though she'd helped to make the wish come true, Eva had a hunch she'd moved down the scale of respect a few notches in Savannah's eyes. "You're very young." Savannah seemed visibly disappointed. "Probably never heard of *Hollywood Squares*, either."

"Oh, that I've heard of." Eva sounded relieved and proud even to herself, but she secretly credited late nights as a new mother pacing with a fussy baby while watching retro TV. Otherwise, she wouldn't have had a clue. She glanced at her watch; it was time to move things along. "So, Savannah, it's a pleasure to meet you, and I must say you look lovely."

The woman's expression changed from baffled-by-someone-who'd-never-heard-of-Nipsey-Russell to abundantly pleased. "I haven't gotten this dolled up in a decade." She patted her beauty salon comb-out that showed distinct outlines of curler marks, all sprayed into place.

"Well, you look beautiful."

Savannah wore what qualified as a grandmother-of-the-bride outfit for an afternoon wedding. A teal-colored chiffon dress with a sequin-and-lace three-quarter-sleeved coordinated jacket. Accessorized with large costume jewelry earrings and matching necklace, most likely crystal. Oh, and a bracelet, too, Eva realized when Savannah scratched her nose in response to the compliment. "You think so?"

"Absolutely. And it's so nice to finally meet you in person." Nipsey had quieted down and Eva dared to take a step closer to clutch and shake Savannah's cool and bony hands.

The woman looked into Eva's eyes, emotion swirling around in her cloudy gray orbs. "I can't tell you how much this means to me."

"You are so welcome. Dreams Come True is honored to grant your wish." Eva wrinkled her nose, fighting off misting up.

"And it's a good one, too!" Savannah went on, her eyes brimming. She let go of Eva's hands to rub her nose, sniff, then noticeably toughen up. All business again. "Joe Aguirre seems like a throwback in time. A good-guy politician who is willing to roll up his sleeves and work for the people of the community, not only for himself. Not to mention he's a fine specimen of a man." She made a hubba-hubba face. "He not only reminds me of Jack Kennedy as a politician, but Sergio Franchi, the handsome Italian singer. Have you met Mayor Aguirre?"

After tonight, Eva needed to google the Italian singer from yesteryear to compare. "Not yet, but we're going to take care of that tonight, right?"

"I feel like Cinderella." Savannah clapped her hands together. "I'm so nervous. I can't wait!"

"Well, our car and driver await. Shall we go?"

Savannah bent to speak to Nipsey. "You be a good boy while Momma's away, you hear me?"

The dog yipped and did its twirling bit again. It made Eva smile, and she had to admit the dog named for a comedian from the last century was cute.

Everything was arranged. Joe Aguirre had agreed to meet Eva and Savannah at the Four Seasons Santa Barbara resort restaurant. As arranged, he'd take a cab over, so later the chauffeur would drive, and Joe could walk Savannah to her door at the end of the evening.

As the driver helped Savannah—who hadn't stopped talking the entire ride—out of the small limousine, Eva scanned the area for any guy in a suit. Her eyes stopped abruptly on a striking man who resembled the pictures she'd seen online but who seemed more like—just as Savannah had described—a throwback in time.

Those pictures didn't do him justice. A quick shudder made her breasts tighten. Must be chilly, she rationalized the reaction.

From the distance, he grinned and casually waved. Then he started walking over in that slim-cut charcoal suit with a narrow dark tie, *très* European, with thick black hair begging for fingers to dig in. She suddenly wished she'd taken Lacy up on her suggestion to wear the peacock blue dress that fit like a…

A completely different image sprang to mind. Baffled by her full-body response, she tried to shut it down, but prickles started at the sides of her neck, first tickling downward and then working up toward her jaw. In a second, her cheeks would be in full blush. Tonight wasn't about her, it was Savannah's big wish.

Joe walked arrow-straight to Savannah and took her hand, kissed it, then glanced into her eyes and smiled. "It's a pleasure to meet you," he said, with that rugged voice Eva had picked up on the other day on the phone. Though, if he'd had a thick Italian accent, she would have bought that, too. His words said, as if he'd just said that to her while kissing her hand, not Savannah's, Eva got a little dreamy-eyed. Wow, talk about charm.

Snap out of it! You're the chaperone and tonight's

all business. Eva homed her gaze back to the guest of honor, while noting her mouth had gone dry. That was one powerful greeting.

When he pulled the bouquet of flowers from behind his back with a grin, his olive complexion made his teeth sparkly white. The guy was nothing short of a dreamboat. No wonder the guest of honor was so smitten with the man.

Under Joe Aguirre's complete attention, Savannah Schuster was all aflutter, the former chatterbox now tamed, and the image warmed Eva's vicariously palpitating heart.

He offered his arm and Savannah took a breath, straightened her shoulders, then slipped her arm through his, having calmed noticeably, assuming almost a regal air as they strolled toward the entrance.

Hadn't Lacy said something about Joe being quality over fortune?

And if that was how Sergio Franchi smiled and behaved with women, Eva was suddenly his biggest fan.

Chapter Three

Inside the gorgeous restaurant, Eva was immediately impressed by how Mayor Aguirre poured all his attention on Savannah both before and after being seated at their cozy partial booth with chairs. Eva took a chair, leaving the senior to sit with Joe all by herself on the half-moon couch complete with throw pillows. Because it was a mild evening, their party of three was placed by the folding windows that opened onto the patio where a firepit was flaming. Beyond was the Pacific Ocean, making its presence known with the lapping of each wave and a briny scent cresting the warm breeze.

Content with her arrangements, Eva smiled, and

as the evening went on, her smile only got bigger thanks to Joe Aguirre being the perfect gentleman for the guest of honor. When the waiter came to take their drink orders Savannah spoke right up.

"I'll have a champagne cocktail," she said to the waiter before turning to Eva. "Just like Cary Grant and Deborah Kerr had in *An Affair to Remember*."

One more thing to look up on the internet.

"I'll have the same." Joe didn't miss a chivalrous beat. "Do you have pink champagne?"

Savannah's eyes brightened. "That's exactly what Cary Grant said!"

Joe tipped his head in deference, his eyes gentle, tender, if Eva wanted to be exact. "My *abuela* loved the classics. She used to make me watch them with her whenever my parents had to work the night shift."

His sweet reaction whispered over Eva's shoulders and tickled up her neck. Quality over fortune. Plus, who didn't like a man who loved his grandmother? "Then I'll have one, too."

He glanced quickly at Eva as she ordered and the instant their eyes made contact, adrenaline popped and bloomed in her chest. Talk about magnetism. No wonder the guy got elected. But he didn't linger on her; no, he knew exactly why he was there, and his attention went right back to his "date" for the night. After all, he *was* a professional politician.

"That was my all-time favorite tragic romance movie," Savannah said. "I sobbed my eyes out."

"I won't publicly admit to it," he said, lowering his voice, "but I may have wiped an eye a time or two during that one."

Savannah scrunched her shoulders and gave Joe an adoring gaze. "I knew I was right. They don't make men like you anymore."

"Of course, that was prepuberty. I haven't mentioned watching that movie to anyone, not even my best friend. Until you."

The man was suave. Like a polished public figure should be. Why wouldn't he be? He'd had plenty of practice over the last three or four years. He'd probably been grooming for public life since his college days. Probably even high school. She'd bet her car he had his eye on being governor one day. Why stop there, maybe president even!

"I feel honored," Savannah cooed.

He squeezed Savannah's hands, which were folded on the table, and they were off to a fine start talking about old movies for the next several minutes. He had great credentials thanks to his classic-movie-watching granny, too. More and more titles Eva would have to look up on the internet later.

When their drinks arrived, Eva suggested a toast. As they raised their glasses, a photographer materialized from what seemed like ocean mist. Was this a service offered by the restaurant?

Joe squinted and immediately looked toward Savannah. "We can send her away if you'd like." Tonight, Savannah was the center of his universe.

"Oh, Joe, I'd love a picture with you. I'll frame it and hang it on my living room wall."

Though torn over the obvious publicity stunt and what seemed like taking advantage of an old woman, Eva couldn't ignore the happiness on Savannah's face. How could she deny her this moment?

"I was planning to take a picture of you guys on my cell phone anyway."

"Oh, will this cost?" Savannah chimed in.

"Cost is no limit. Don't even give it a thought. That was just my clumsy way of saying, whatever you want, however you want to do it." And oh, why did her eyes catch Joe's at that moment. His amused, teasing gaze implying he may have heard or put a double entendre in her statement.

They all three lifted their glasses, and the photographer, whether official to the restaurant or hired by the mayor's campaign manager, clicked a picture of the couple on the couch, leaving her and her champagne flute out of the frame. Grateful, because Eva felt a delayed reaction from looking into Joe's eyes that second time while saying *whatever you want, however you want to do it.* Her full-on blush didn't need to be recorded for posterity. Even her ears felt warm.

She gave a tiny headshake to clear her brain and

lifted her glass higher after the photo was taken. "To a special night for a one-of-a-kind lady."

Savannah's eyes sparkled and the sight warmed Eva's heart. This was what she loved about her job, giving people these moments to remember. Or in Savannah's case, to hang on to for as long as she could. Another flash went off, this one from an angle including Eva. "May tonight be an affair to remember." She thought she'd been clever tying in the movie title with the toast, then instantly worried that using *affair* instead of *evening* would be construed as another under-the-table hint. Why did the man rile her so?

And a third flash snapped as they clinked their glasses.

Eva watched Savannah sip her cocktail as she also took a drink. Not bad. She'd have to remember this and order it again sometime. Not that she'd have a special occasion like this again soon. From over the top of her champagne flute her glance drifted and got tangled up with Joe's as he took a man-size swallow. There was another click. His eyes crinkled at the sides and it was evident he smiled behind that glass. For the fourth picture, or her? Regardless, there went that pop in her chest again, and she nearly swallowed wrong simply from watching him.

He didn't seem to be putting on an act as she'd originally suspected. The man seemed to be honestly enjoying himself. And all through dinner, Savannah ate up the nonstop attention.

"I need the powder room," Savannah said before dessert, after they'd all shared a harbor seafood platter for starters, followed by hand-cut pasta with Maine lobster, another champagne cocktail and a main course of New York steak and Chilean sea bass with a wine handpicked by Eva. Joe and Savannah kept the conversation flowing freely and naturally, and whatever topic Savannah brought up, Joe seemed to know something, no matter how little, about it. Eva had also dutifully taken a picture of each of the served plates at the guest of honor's request, and she planned to make a small scrapbook to present to Savannah in the coming week.

Though Eva would've loved to grab a moment to herself with Joe—because he'd turned out to be a fascinating guy who knew how to carry an interesting and enjoyable conversation, unlike the men Eva had last dated—she jumped up to help the guest of honor stand, then accompanied her to the ladies' room.

Tonight wasn't about her. It belonged to Savannah. But she'd certainly enjoyed every minute of it. She checked her watch; already it was nearly ten o'clock. Lacy had been right—Noah should spend the night. She sent a quick text saying so as she waited for Savannah to finish in the stall.

"I'm having the time of my life," Savannah said a few moments later in front of the restroom mirror, aiming a lipstick at a pair of nearly nonexistent lips.

Lacy had sent a thumbs-up sign in reply to her

text, and Eva was surprised by her sense of relief. Her boy was in good hands. She didn't have to rush to him tonight. Suddenly, an odd feeling came over her: she was without a care in the world.

"I've never had such a fancy meal in my life," Savannah said, blotting her lips on tissue paper.

Eva fought the urge to hug the woman who was so genuine and sweet. Had she really never had a meal like this? It put Eva's privileged history in perspective, because fancy dining had been a way of life growing up. Something this hardworking onetime secretary who was currently primping her stiff hair before the mirror couldn't relate to. And admittedly Eva had not even enjoyed it much back then, just taken it for granted. Nothing like tonight.

Life was crazy that way. Like a twin sister showing up after thirty-one years.

With being watched by his grandmother while parents were working the local farms, Joe Aguirre probably hadn't had many meals like this, either. And Lacy probably hadn't experienced food like this until she was serving it at the local fancy restaurant where she began her career. The new perspective brought in a wave of guilt. But the truth was, she'd been a lonely child growing up and all the fancy meals in the world couldn't change that.

"Well, let's go have dessert, then!" On a bittersweet note, Eva guided Savannah back toward the dining room.

* * *

Joe's phone buzzed again, annoyingly, in his pocket. He didn't need to look to know who it was. He had skipped checking after the first one, when all Mike asked was How's it going? As far as he was concerned, the night was his. He was off duty from being mayor, unless a major earthquake or flash fire occurred.

Savannah and Eva had gone to the ladies' room, and Joe ignored Mike's text, choosing instead to gaze at the stars, to inhale the scent and listen to the ocean. Tonight had been a surprising gift shared with a spunky senior citizen and a mystery woman who knew how to hide in the shadows for her client's sake. Though he sensed she was on the ready if the conversation ever lulled, which it hadn't. Not for one minute. He and Savannah had really hit it off, thanks in no small part to her engaging personality and his fondness for his *abuela*.

How often did he get the chance to simply relax and enjoy himself these days? Especially in such a swanky restaurant. And with such good company who only wanted to get to know *him*, who didn't want or need anything from him. A refreshing change.

He'd also changed his view on spoiled rich girls, thanks to the generosity of Eva's nonprofit. Great ideas deserved recognition. Rich didn't automatically mean spoiled, just different, and he chastised himself for stereotyping. Rich was different from him, that was for sure.

As he stared at the night sky, thoughts free flowing, an image of a perfectly placed and feminine cleft in Eva's chin edged out the stars. That website picture wasn't touched up like he'd thought; in fact, it didn't nearly do her justice. Perplexed, he shook his head to get back on track.

He'd enjoyed the evening as much as Savannah appeared to. For eighty-four, she was full of life and conversation. The woman knew her baseball, too. Go Dodgers.

And here they came, at the exact time dessert was being served, which prevented him from enjoying watching Eva saunter—and there really was no other way to describe her walk—toward the table. Though he'd still grabbed a satisfying glance at the curve of her calves. Liked how her heels highlighted the muscle. Yeah, she went to the gym. Or maybe in her case, had a home gym.

"I never want the night to end," Savannah said, showing the first signs of being a little tipsy.

From across the room, Eva watched Joe at the table, waiting. He hadn't taken the free time to multitask; his cell was nowhere in sight. It was another thing she liked about him. He simply sat on the comfy couch and watched the ocean, a mild expression of contentment on his face.

"Then let's take our time with dessert and order coffee, and we'll talk as long as you want."

"What'd I order for dessert again?"

He must have sensed they were coming, because he jumped up and moved to meet them.

It was the first time Savannah also showed a sign of forgetting anything. Considering the two cocktails and the wine with dinner, Eva could understand. She was feeling more than a little buzzed herself.

"We ordered a dessert platter, so we can sample a bit of everything."

"That's right, the works," Joe added, holding out his arm for Savannah to take and guiding her the rest of the way back to the table. Eva followed.

"Oh, that's right. I get dibs on the chocolate cake."

Eva didn't recall anything about chocolate cake, but if anything on the platter looked chocolate, she'd be sure to pass it to Savannah. Because it was her night, and Joe Aguirre had made sure to make Savannah feel like the most special woman on the planet.

Wow, what would it be like to have his undivided attention showered on her? As she imagined just that, Eva's full-body tingles found their way to some extremely interesting places. Too far-fetched to visualize, the two of them tearing each other's clothes off, so she'd keep her little fantasy of crawling all over that fine body to herself. But man, did her cheeks feel flushed.

* * *

After dessert and coffee were served, Joe shared a bite of key lime something or other with Eva as Savannah dug into caramel sea salt ice cream covered in a dark chocolate shell. It wasn't cake, but she appeared satisfied. Where he'd give Savannah a thumbs-up for knowing how to live in the moment and enjoy her dessert, Eva's delicate bites—the way her mouth, the bottom lip twice as plump as the upper, curled around the spoon—were far more intriguing. Watching her take a small portion of the dessert from a spot he'd just sampled, and put it between those lips, obviously savoring the tangy flavor that still lingered on *his* tongue, seemed both intimate and downright sexy.

He wondered what might happen, under different circumstances, with this thing that seemed apparent to him between them. Was it all his imagination?

Too soon, the coffee service was done, decaf all around, and it appeared all the goodness of the meal had settled in. The guest of honor yawned. Didn't try to hide it because no way could a hand cover the size of that contented gape, complete with what seemed like surround sound effects.

"All good things must come to an end, right, Savannah?" he said, patting her hand.

With post-yawn teary eyes, she nodded, a sad expression on her face. "I never was the life of a party, could never stay up that late."

Probably because she'd been a hard worker all her life. The salt of the earth, just like his parents.

"Well, you've been a great companion tonight. I've enjoyed every minute." It came from his heart. From the corner of his eye he saw Eva reach for her purse. His gut told him to let it be, but he'd had such a great time with two amazing women that he felt compelled. "May I cover this? Or at least help?"

Eva looked appalled. Not what he'd predicted. "No. This is one hundred percent covered by Dreams Come True."

He knew when to hold and when to fold, and now was not the time to stand on principle. So he tipped his head and remained silent, forcing back the protest in his egalitarian thoughts. He'd gladly pay for the night under different circumstances. He'd also be sure to make a substantial donation to her charity.

While Eva took care of business, he helped Savannah gather her purse and get her sea legs back. Dessert and coffee had helped some.

"What about those pictures we took?" she asked.

As though on cue, the young woman with the camera popped out from around the corner. Had she been crouching and hiding? He tensed when she appeared.

"If you don't mind," the photographer said, "we'd like to run this picture in the *Little River Valley Voice*." She showed Savannah and Joe the chosen photograph, just the two of them. Only Savannah smiled as his gut tightened. "But I need some information first."

Was this all a publicity stunt for Dreams Come True? A useful little tool to raise awareness of her company? A pat on her back, shared with the entire town of Little River Valley? A great way to solicit contributions? Sure Mike had signed on, said it would be good for the campaign, but as far as Joe was concerned, he'd been a private citizen tonight.

Eva finished paying the bill and tossed him a concerned and questioning look at the exact moment he lobbed his suspicious stare.

Then the setup finally computed. Who was looking to gain from the evening the most? Dreams Come True or his reelection campaign? Mike!

"I had no ulterior motives," Eva said in response to his stare. "I was granting a wish. That's all. My organization doesn't need publicity."

"And I didn't know anything about the pictures and the article, I swear," he said.

She glared at him. He stared back. He'd spent enough time with her to sense she was telling the truth. All he could hope for was that she could do the same with him. Her accusing eyes relaxed. Good. A solid truce.

The phone vibrating in his pants pocket didn't let up. This time it was a call. Angry, he dug it out and answered. Mike.

"I got us a spot in the Saturday afternoon newspaper," his micromanaging best friend and campaign manager said.

"You should've consulted me first," he hissed, seething.

"I tried! You weren't responding."

"I'd be thrilled to get my picture in the paper," Savannah blurted. "This is the biggest thing to happen to me since I retired." The guest of honor weighed in, immediately quelling the last of the blame in Eva's eyes.

"Are you sure? Because this isn't part of the deal at all," Eva said, her only concern obviously for Savannah. She must be putting her contempt for Joe on standby.

"It didn't go unnoticed that, though Mayor Aguirre is running for reelection, he didn't bring up the subject for one second tonight," Savannah continued. "All he seemed to be interested in was me. What politician on this planet is like that? Shouldn't the guy get some credit? A shout-out from the *Voice*?"

Left with diluted aspersions, Eva seemed to change from tense to understanding in record time. Good. She wasn't a grudge holder. Something else Joe liked about her, besides the way she filled out that little black dress. Not to mention the color of her hair. And those pale blue eyes. He could go on but it might get him in trouble.

While Savannah talked her head off with the reporter, Joe went to flag down the chauffeur. He needed a break because he was full of mixed-up feelings about Eva. Some hot and edgy, others extremely cautious. A few deep breaths of fresh air were in order.

Within another five minutes, the ladies exited the restaurant to the awaiting limo. A car with enough room for a group of six to easily stretch their legs and relax. With tinted windows all around and a darkened divider between the driver and the passengers. He'd also discovered a chilled bottle of champagne ready and waiting in an ice bucket.

Nice driver service.

Because it was there, Eva, Joe and Savannah partook of one last glass of champagne on the drive back to the senior assisted-living apartments in Little River Valley. Now Joe stood with Savannah at her door, with noticeably no barking from the other side. Must be past Nipsey's bedtime.

"This was one of the best nights of my life," Savannah said, looking up into Joe's benevolent face. "Definitely the best since I turned sixty."

"I can't remember when I've had such a good time, either," he said, "Thank *you*."

"Thank me? For what?"

"For being you. One great lady."

She melted against him with a hug. He easily hugged back. The man was a natural, nothing practiced or slick about him.

"I'm going to follow your campaign and tell all my neighbors to vote for you. That Barnstable lady isn't for the seniors. You are."

"Thank you, but that's not necessary. How about we just email, and I'll call to check in from time to time? See how you're doing."

"I'd love that. Thank you for making this old woman the happiest girl in the world tonight."

With that, Joe placed his hands on both sides of Savannah's face and kissed her forehead. She closed her eyes and let several seconds go by as she obviously savored her special kiss.

"Good night, Savannah Schuster. I'll be in touch," he said with the kindest smile Eva had ever seen. In her heart she knew it wasn't an empty promise; he would keep in touch.

The guy was unlike any public figure she'd ever met. Not to mention he filled out his suit to perfection, and that hair, OMG. Did Savannah want to run her fingers through it as badly as she did? But the sweetheart simply stood there all dreamy-eyed. Talk about a wasted opportunity. Up until now, hadn't she been a perfect lesson on living in the moment?

Ha! Like Eva would take an opportunity with him if given the chance. Since becoming a mother, she'd catered to her son, putting his needs first, not hers. And those needs had been seriously building up over the past year. Being around a guy like Joe had forced her to remember how much she missed getting close to a man…making love.

She patted her hair. This line of thinking had to stop.

The night and drinks had obviously caught up to Eva. Where Joe Aguirre was concerned, though he was only a mayor of a small city in California, through his actions with Savannah tonight, he'd become nothing short of a prince.

And she was a soppy-eyed, sex-starved goner.

They exited the building in silence. Anything they said would only ruin that wonderful moment filled with the satisfaction of seeing a woman transfixed by having her dream come true, after being diagnosed with dementia. But when they got to the limousine and the driver opened the door, Joe took Eva's hand to help her inside. It was the first time they'd touched all night, and the warmth of his palm and fingers shimmered through her.

She swallowed and dared to look into his eyes. He'd felt something, too. There was no doubt about his heated stare.

They sat side by side on the leather bench seat toward the back of the limo. The lights were dimmed, and the skylight had been opened. Completely blocked out in the front, the driver started the engine and drove off. A satisfying hum from the road beneath the seats matched the hum vibrating through her.

Fresh sea air infused the interior, but it didn't clear

her thoughts. The stars and the moon passed overhead. That was more in keeping with her mood. She kicked off her shoes. Joe noticed. He gestured toward the bottle of champagne. She declined. Why toy with the perfection of this moment?

"It was great meeting Savannah. Thank you."

"You're entirely welcome."

"But now I'd like to get to know more about you."

She sighed. Tonight had been all about fulfilling a person's wish, a dream coming true. It had been wonderful and exciting and...

"Do we really want to drop back into reality already?"

He looked perplexed but intrigued.

"Tonight was about granting a wish. Living a fantasy. Savannah got to have dinner with a smart and sexy man. She's probably still walking on clouds."

"And here we are riding in a limousine on a beautiful night," he said, completely understanding her line of thinking. "Why blow the chance of a lifetime?"

"Exactly. Let's just stay in the moment." Yes, thanks to Savannah, she would dare to say it. This, right now, with him, was her dream, too.

His gaze didn't leave her face as he took her hand again and lifted it toward his mouth, tenderly kissing it, as he had Savannah's forehead, but in her case the frisson skipped up her arm, across her chest, then straight to her woman parts.

"Thank you for tonight," he said in that deep and now husky voice.

She could barely breathe. With a single touch and a kiss to her hand, he'd just managed to knock her over the head with lust.

"You're welcome," she whispered, and then, taking the biggest chance of her life, added, "And thank you for now."

One eyebrow shot up. He was a quick study, but she wanted to be sure.

"This magical night. We can make it ours now."

She'd given him a less than subtle go-ahead. He moved toward her, taking the time to study her face up close, his eyes revealing how much he liked what he saw. She froze under his spell, barely able to breathe, but she'd just bragged about making magic. He was too much of a gentleman to overstep a silent invitation, he'd proved that already.

Did she have the nerve to go for her dream tonight? To make love to a sexy and amazing man in a limousine? No strings. Just feeling and being. Together. Stealing these few moments left in the night for herself?

She swallowed again, followed her instinct, took his face in her hands and kissed him with everything she had. The contact with his mouth made her woozy. His quick inhale and welcoming response fed the fire lapping her insides. Of course, he was a great kisser. How could the man not be, with such appeal oozing from every pore?

His hands slowly traveled all over her, their kisses deepened and fed some of the hunger welling up, but not nearly enough, and mostly stirring up more. Somehow her skirt got hiked up and she straddled him. To hell with twisting and turning, she needed to be facing him. Thankfully she'd skipped nylons. Heat from his palms pressed on her hips, pushing her closer to him.

Within moments clothes got unbuttoned and opened, and her breasts, though still in her bra, were flush to his chest. Nothing could stop them now.

"We're at Mayor Aguirre's home," the chauffeur said through the intercom.

Eva stopped dead, looked into Joe's fired-up eyes, his hair disheveled and begging for her fingers to return. He was right there with her, wanting what she wanted. She pressed her breathless lips to his again for one more quick taste, then snuggled closer to his chest, his hands pushing her hips firmly on top of his lap.

Somehow, she managed to find the intercom button.

"Keep driving!" they said in unison.

Chapter Four

The next week

"Look at these poll numbers!" Mike Machado said, pacing in front of Joe's desk and flapping the local rag in his face with each pass. "That Wish Come True date was a huge success."

"*Dreams* Come True," Joe corrected. "Let me see that." He leaned forward and, on the next pass, snatched the newspaper out of Mike's hand. One look at the numbers, and he sat straighter. "My lead is over five percent?"

Mike folded his arms over his paunch, gave a self-satisfied nod. "Yeah, and three weeks ago you were practically nose-to-nose with Louella. My goal is to make it double digits."

Joe handed the paper back. "You think it was because of the story they ran in the *Voice*?"

"Absolutely. Savannah Schuster even wrote a letter to the editor singing your praises. We need to get that lady on the stump with us."

But that would entail contacting Eva again. Eva, who'd made him promise that what they'd done in that limousine after taking Savannah home would never be spoken of or happen again. Her reason? She was too busy. Join the club! He was busy, too, running for reelection while serving as mayor. But she'd made her point clear. Neither of them was in the right place to start something.

They should have thought of that *before* they'd started what they had...which, wow, sure was something amazing. He hadn't gotten that hot and wild with a woman since, well, since never! The whole mutual seduction in a limousine bit was completely out of character. And he'd certainly never covered anything close to the uncharted territory he had with Eva in a limousine before, or with anyone else. The absolute best thing was, she'd started it.

They'd been fueled by champagne and good deeds. That was his side of the story and he was sticking to it. Because the thought of making a woman like Eva a part of his world was out of the question. He was a hardworking lawyer/mayor of a very small town, running for reelection with a salary to match. She lived in that incredible place in Santa Barbara—he knew because he'd insisted the driver take her home first. It was the gentlemanly thing to do. The least he could do after that crazy back-seat romp.

Though he'd spent several hours earlier that night being the perfect Cary Grant in *An Affair to Remember*, the last hour-plus alone with Eva in the back of that stretch limo had been more *Tarzan, King of the Jungle* with Jane.

"Wait, what are you doing?" Joe snapped out of his wildly vivid thoughts in time to see Mike making a call.

"I'm asking Savannah to come to your rally at Oakland Bowl tomorrow."

The famous bowl-shaped stage smack in the middle of an oak grove and park in the center of town was the perfect venue for his daytime political assemblies. It could seat close to a thousand people, with room enough for blankets and chairs in the surrounding park, and he hoped to reach more and more of the town voters there to make his case in person.

At night the bowl hosted a full calendar of entertainment events ranging from classical music to classic rock and roll, with poetry and art conferences in between. Truth was, if he was lucky the bowl would be half-full tomorrow. Things had slowed down on the excitement scale. What would Louella Barnstable think of next?

"I'm not sure about that call, man." He didn't want to come off as using Savannah. That was the last thing he wanted to do.

"I am." Mike held his finger in the air to shut Joe up. "Let's let Savannah decide for herself."

"She's in early dementia. She shouldn't be making decisions like that on her own."

"Give the woman some credit. She asked to have dinner with you, a perfect levelheaded wish, right? Oh, hello, is this Ms. Schuster?" Mike took a breath. "This is Mayor Aguirre's campaign manager, Mike Machado, and I wanted to personally invite you to the Aguirre for Mayor rally at Oakland Bowl tomorrow at noon."

Mike paused, listening for several seconds. "Understandable. Well, we hope to see you there. If you do come, please see me and I'll get you a spot right up front."

Joe shot up from his chair, radically shaking his head no!

There went Mike's "shush" finger again. "Fabulous. I look forward to meeting you."

"What did you do?" Joe came around the desk and stared Mike in the face, who looked annoyingly pleased with himself.

"I invited an avid supporter to your rally. She told me she'd been talking to all the people at her assisted-living facility about what a great mayor you are. She even offered to hold a sign." Mike snapped his fingers. "Do we have signs? Are your high school volunteers making them?"

"That's your department, remember?" The sinking feeling in Joe's stomach bled throughout his body. It simply seemed wrong to use Savannah's affection for him to his advantage, a sentiment obviously not held by his campaign manager.

The next day was perfect weatherwise—midseventies, sunny with only a mild breeze. Who wouldn't want to be outdoors on a Saturday like that?

The Oakland Bowl turnout was far better than Joe had hoped for, yet only filled half the seats under the incomplete canopy of ancient oak branches. The early birds spread out around the nine hundred green-colored seats, talking robustly amongst themselves in the dappled shade. Joe recognized several faces and waved hello.

The election was two months away and most folks were still happily oblivious about the upcoming event, paying little attention to the issues. Only the diehards kept up. He checked his watch; twenty minutes to go. Things could still change, but so far Joe didn't see any difference in public support since the Make-A-Wish senior version had taken place. Nor had he seen an increase in donations. Maybe Mike knew something he didn't.

Mike paced the stage in ill-fitting khakis like a caged animal, making Joe nervous. All Joe wanted to do was talk to the people and let them know he intended to continue running the city like he always had. He also hoped to convince them the city would be just fine without outside commerce invading their town. Of course, he'd be preaching to the choir, with most of the crowd already being those who supported him. He waved and smiled at several other people he recognized from the community. He hoped the spectacle in the park would bring curious people over from their Saturday shopping to see what the deal was, and he might earn a new vote or two. A sitting mayor could only hope.

The local public electric bus pulled to the curb on Main Street and soon a long line of seniors filtered out. Terrific! Maybe Savannah had recruited neighbors from her residence.

He looked closer. Ah, great, someone was handing each of them a sign as they got off. More specifically, a little lady with long silver hair worn in her signature milkmaid braids gave out Change the Charter signs. Louella Barnstable had obviously orchestrated this cagey move.

Suddenly, the thought of sweet Savannah coming and sitting on the stage with him didn't seem like such a bad idea. He scribbled a few notes on his prepared speech, thoughts about asking the local diners and cafés to extend a generous discount to the over-sixty-five crowd for breakfast. And why not lunch, too? Just as quickly, he scratched it out. That wouldn't be wise; he'd have to run it by the local small business owners first, before broaching the topic in public today.

Why didn't he think of this sooner? One thing he'd learned early in life about campaign promises—don't make one you can't keep! Voters had long memories about such things.

He glanced up in time to see a familiar face coming toward him. One who obviously hadn't just gotten off the bus. The friendly visage of none other than Savannah Schuster in a wide-brimmed straw hat—apparently thinking she'd be out in the glaring noon sun and not under the bowl of the Oakland stage—wearing a bright yellow shirt and baggy white pants.

"Yoo-hoo!" She waved and picked up her pace. He waved back, happy to see her. Impressed with how quickly she could move.

Someone followed behind, and that someone was not nearly as affable in nature. No yoo-hoos or waves. Nope. Eva DeLongpre's smile was tight and forced and didn't come anywhere near her eyes as she accompanied his recent Dreams Come True date toward the stage. Still, the mere sight of her wearing cropped tan pants with a peach wraparound top let loose a flock of memories. Like blackbirds at dusk flying in murmurations, swirling and pulsating the thoughts set free inside his brain. Intense flashbacks of sexy positions, the touch of silken skin, musky scents. Before he knew it, he was the victim of a sudden gust of full-body cravings. Wow, what had they done.

Then, as if he was the recipient of a sucker punch, Joe took a step back, the wind knocked out of him. Eva also carried a baby on her hip.

When she'd said what they'd done in the back of that limousine was a one-off, she'd obviously had a good reason.

Sweat beaded on his upper lip. Was she married? Oh man, just what he didn't need during the reelection, to be accused of an affair with a married woman! Obviously, she was or had been involved with someone, though. Funny that topic hadn't come up that night at dinner or in the limo. Not once.

Another thought occurred, making his forehead go moist. He'd thought Eva looked just like Zack Gardner's fiancée, Lacy. Could she have played a trick on him? But why? Who cared, if that was the case. Holy crap. What had he done?

Talk about the "hardest thing ever" to-do list. Eva couldn't very well turn down Savannah's request to bring her to the Oakland Bowl rally for her newest friend, the mayor. With her memory loss issues, it wouldn't be safe for Savannah to attend anything unaccompanied, so Eva had offered to drive her here after delivering the scrapbook she'd made for her. Under normal circumstances it wouldn't be Eva's responsibility—she didn't live in the same town even—but she'd honestly felt she and Savannah had become friends on their special dinner out. And if it wasn't for the nonprofit, Savannah would never have met and had dinner with Joe.

Flushing hot with who knew what—embarrassment...remaining lust from the other night?—Eva followed Savannah down the center aisle of seats with Noah on her hip and the baby bag on the opposite shoulder, a strained smile pasted on her face. When she saw Joe standing on that stage, she tensed. He was dressed in jeans, a plaid button-up shirt neatly pressed and with sleeves rolled to his forearms—a sure sign he was working for the people. He didn't have cross-trainers on as she'd expected, but Western boots. How well she remembered those narrow hips. The "never again" guy was too bleeping appealing.

Her biggest irritation about having a redhead's pale complexion was she'd have to face the man she'd gotten way up close and very personal with while fighting off a major blush. Still, they'd done some amazing things in the back of that limousine; if there was ever something worth blushing over, that would be it. Had she gone temporarily crazy that night? It had been the last thing she'd ever expected to do, and she was still trying to straighten out in her mind their impulsive night together. There simply was no explanation. Other than Joe and how unpretentious and utterly appealing he'd been. And how she'd fallen for him.

"Savannah!" Joe said, clearly surprised about the two of them showing up, or maybe just her? "Wonderful to see you."

Like old friends, Joe opened his arms and Savannah stepped right in for a hug until the brim of her hat hit him in the jaw. Clearly embarrassed, she chuckled, and Joe tipped his head in a how-cute-are-you expression.

"Eva was good enough to bring me. I might still be wandering around Main Street otherwise." Savannah snickered, but Eva sensed she was being brutally honest. Forgetting one's keys or misplacing glasses was one thing, but not knowing how to find the way home meant a whole new level of memory issues. Eva suspected Savannah wasn't there yet, not with her ability to spout off entire casts from classic movies, but she didn't want to take any chances with her alone in the streets. Savannah was wise enough to agree. "You should see the scrapbook she made of our date."

"I'd love to. Hello, Eva," Joe said in a more serious tone.

Eva tried to tamp down her body's reaction; she didn't want to read into it, but seriously, how could she not? They'd taken a trip to the moon and back together. She couldn't let herself think about that or she'd go all tingly again. "Hi, Joe." She avoided his eyes, glancing instead around the bowl. "Looks like a good turnout."

"About what I expected." He pointed toward the back, to Main Street, where the seniors walked back and forth with their signs, respectfully not stepping onto the Oakland Bowl area, but making clear their point about the charter. "Except for that."

She looked over her shoulder, switching Noah to the other hip to do so. He squirmed but adjusted to the lopsided change without too much griping, what with the baby bag now crowding him out. "Yeah, we noticed on our way in." Since they hadn't talked a single sentence of politics on the dinner out, she wasn't up-to-date with the issues. "What's up?"

"My opponent thinks we need to let a fast-food chain build in town so people Savannah's age can have a cheap breakfast out. Which means changing the town charter that has been in place for over sixty years."

"Ah, which would open the door to all kinds of other chains wanting in, too. I see."

"Bingo. Who's this little guy?" His quick change of the subject meant Joe clearly couldn't avoid the obvious for another moment.

She sucked a breath. "This is my son, Noah."

"Hey, Noah," Joe said, a gentle if perplexed smile creasing his face.

Noah, who looked far closer to Joe's coloring than hers, pumped his pudgy legs and swatted with his hand. His version of a wave hello. "Fflurrt. Mep."

"Not only is Eva an amazing wish-granter, but she is also a wonderful adoptive mother," Savannah chimed in, sounding anything but forgetful about their conversation on the drive in.

Yes, that was the deal. *My son is adopted.* Why did he look relieved? For all he knew she could still be married. "Uh, a single mother?"

Okay, the lawyer in him went to a direct line of questioning. "Yes." She tipped her head to accentuate her current state of relationship.

His eyebrows smoothed. "Both admirable and, I suspect, challenging." His look of approval made her tense mood brighten; this time his smile was genuine.

"You got that second part right," she said, putting Noah down and holding his hands as he attempted to walk unsteadily back up the aisle.

"Hi! I'm Mike Machado, the mayor's campaign manager. Here, have a pin and a bumper sticker." He offered both to Savannah, since Eva's hands were full. The sticker read Mayor Joe Aguirre, Locally Grown, Promising to Keep Little River Valley Sustainable. "Barnstable only moved here after she retired in Los Angeles." Mike further explained in hushed tones, "Wants to make the place like her old neighborhood instead of appreciating what she got away from."

Savannah immediately put the button pin on her collar. Eva held back, worrying Noah might get pricked by the pin but planned to put the bumper sticker on the car before they left today. "Thanks."

Half a dozen youths fanned out amid the crowd handing out the goodies, and Eva wondered if they were even old enough to vote. A small band of musicians, who also looked no older than seniors in high school, began to play on the stage with an electric piano, bass and drums. Joe certainly had the youth support.

"Okay, Joe. Time to make your speech," Mike said. "Hey, Savannah, will you do us the honor of joining us on the stage?"

Looking like a classic Cheshire cat, Savannah followed him. "The honor is mine." She turned and waved Eva on. "Come on. Join us."

Alarmed, Eva didn't move. Joe's gaze found hers, and she was sure he also looked concerned. But how could she say no and keep her eye out for Savannah. It would be easy to get lost in a crowd of several hundred afterward. Get lost while wearing a wide-brimmed canvas hat and a bright yellow smock? Eva chuckled to herself. Still, she followed.

Mike set out three extra folding chairs, and as Eva sat, she worried Noah might get restless, make a spectacle of himself and distract from Joe's message.

She got out her emergency graham cracker pack and his sippy cup of water hoping for the best, impatiently waiting for the rally to begin.

More people filtered into the empty seats as the band wound down their catchy tune. Joe didn't wait for an introduction, just went directly to the microphone and began a low-key speech that sounded more like a casual chat with a big group of friends. The guy was a natural.

Halfway through his message about what he'd done as mayor and what he hoped to do if reelected, the seniors, under Louella Barnstable's lead, began their chant. "Change the Charter! Change the Charter!"

Mike immediately hopped off the stage and headed toward them, but Joe spoke before Mike could make a scene.

"I understand that our senior population is growing in town, which is a great thing. In fact, I signed off on the hundred new cottages for seniors over sixty just last year. We welcome people in Little River Valley, all people, but here's the thing. We also honor our town charter. Bringing in big company chains, especially fast-food restaurants and brandname stores, was specifically addressed from the beginning. Our city said no, thank you, then, and out of respect for their wisdom, I'm saying that again now. Changing the charter to allow them isn't the fix for our citizens on fixed incomes and won't make anything better."

To that the group chanted louder.

Joe raised his voice. "Instead of changing the law and the future of Little River Valley, why not change our approach to how we do business now? If the issue is access to affordable food, we can meet the needs of every person in our community if we put our heads together and figure it out…without changing the charter." The audience responded with applause, drowning out the chanters. Eva joined in. That was one good speech.

At this point, Noah got restless, wanting to get down and crawl. Eva went for another emergency snack stored in the baby bag—Kix corn puffs. Out they came, and she doled them out one at a time, settling the previously antsy kid into a contented baby. Eva hoped the snack would last until Joe had finished talking.

"I have some ideas that I plan to bring up in my speech next week for the Rotary Club. I also intend to write an op-ed for the *Voice* addressing this issue. In the meantime, please tell your friends about Mayor Joe. And to the folks in the back, good for you for exercising your constitutional rights as citizens. We'll keep this discussion going. I promise. Oh, and be sure to grab your Vote for Joe button before you leave." That drew a good laugh from the crowd, even a few of the sign-holding seniors way in the back.

"And remember, I'm Joe Aguirre, locally grown and promising to keep Little River Valley sustainable." The tension Eva had stored up over the small confrontation and Noah's fidgeting released. Until Savannah stood up and began a chant of her own.

"Seniors vote for Joe! Seniors vote for Joe!" She gestured as if she was a church choir director. A handful of older people in the crowd half-heartedly joined in, but soon after, everyone else repeated the phrase. Many more stood, once again drowning out the organized group in the back. And thankfully, also covering the unhappy squeals from Noah.

At the end of Savannah's group chant, over half the crowd stood and applauded for Joe's speech. Eva hadn't failed to notice that the same photographer from the other night at the restaurant had been popping up from behind bushes and trees, from behind the stage, and just about every possible angle in the audience during the rally and taking pictures, no doubt for the *Little River Valley Voice.*

Eva stood back as Savannah said goodbye to Joe, giving her heartfelt support and promising to do whatever she could to help.

"I'll meet you down there," Eva said, gathering Noah and heading down the bowl stairs to the area in front of the stage. She avoided saying goodbye to Joe herself, using the excuses of her son and needing to deliver Savannah home. The torn look on Joe's face didn't go unnoticed. Did he want to talk to her

alone? Not a good idea. What happened the other
night couldn't happen again. What he did to her and
her good sense was far too dangerous. As amazing
as they were together, she didn't have time to deal
with such things now. Not in this new-mommy-who-
runs-a-business and first-time-homeowner stage.

Trying not to make Savannah uncomfortable by
watching her like a hawk, Eva glanced toward the
receding crowd, seeing another redhead coming her
way.

"How did I not see you?" Eva asked as Lacy came
grinning up the aisle.

"We were off on the side, in the park, where
Emma and her friend could toss the Frisbee."

With evidence of their seating arrangements, two
lawn chairs in each hand, Zack walked behind. "Hey,
Eva. I didn't know you were one of Joe's VIPs."

VIP? The idea it renewed made her cringe. Why
had she agreed to sit on the stage? "Uh, Savannah
is the lady of the hour, and I am merely her chauffeur and chaperone."

"I see." Zack leaned the chairs against the stage.
"I'm going to see if I can grab his ear for a sec." Off
he went, taking the stage stairs two at a time.

Savannah wandered toward the edge of the stage,
and Zack took her hand and helped her down the first
and second steps until she proved she was good to
go on alone.

"Can you come for a barbecue later?" Lacy asked. "I have something I'd like to talk to you about."

"Of course. After I take Savannah home and let Noah nap, I'll come back."

"He can nap at my house. It's quiet there."

"But won't you be spending the afternoon at Zack's?"

"Yes, but why should you drive all the way home to Santa Barbara and come back again?"

"Because that's where I live? And Noah sleeps best in his crib?" Occasionally Lacy pushed Eva a bit further than she was comfortable with, like right now. She and Noah had a routine and changing it to meet Lacy's needs wasn't an option.

"Okay, I get it. We'll talk more about this later."

Savannah arrived and Eva introduced her to Lacy. "My word, you two are doubles!"

Eva and Lacy beamed at each other. They'd never get tired of the effect they had on people the first time they saw them together.

Noah was squirming beyond the point where Eva could hold him any longer. She bent and let him down and he made a beeline for Emma, who'd just shown up with her friend from the park. Going right to her, Noah let Emma pick him up to say hello. Then she and her friend each took one of his hands and let him walk-stumble on the park grass.

"By the way," Savannah continued, "I told Joe we'd be at his next rally. I forget where he said it would be, but it's a Saturday." She stopped, looking mildly perplexed. "I think that's what he said."

As Eva's stomach twisted and dropped, she did her best not to panic while she did the math, two weeks from today. Savannah didn't understand Joe was the last person Eva wanted to spend time with, and she wasn't about to explain why now. But she gazed into the woman's eyes and saw the joy, how being a part of Joe's campaign made her happy. Eva bit her tongue on her first honest response, *Find your own ride over*, instead saying, "That should work for me. I'm not sure how happy that will make Noah, though."

"I can watch him," Lacy offered without a single moment's thought.

"The baby was a big hit!" Mike Machado appeared from out of nowhere. "I just heard Savannah's coming to the next Little River Valley High School track rally, and I wanted to beg you to bring your son. To show three generations on the stage with Joe. Seniors, the current residents, and our future, is a great example of what Mayor Aguirre stands for."

What would he say if he knew she didn't even live in Little River Valley? Could that damage the campaign?

Two seniors approached Savannah and began a side conversation with her as Eva kept track of her whereabouts and Noah's. Things were certainly getting complicated.

"I guess it's better he gets a little exercise before we drive home" was all Eva could think to say. Thankfully, Mike had moved on to shake hands with another group of people. Zack and Joe were still talking.

"Never hurts," Lacy said. "Though since I've never been a mom, I can only guess."

"Can I bring anything later?" Eva said, happy to get back to a topic she had some control over.

"Zack has everything covered. Just know I have something I'd like to discuss with you."

"Sounds serious. Should I be scared?"

"With me? Never."

Eva figured it would be about the need to get in touch with her mom on her world tour. They had so many questions about the unusual adoption that had separated twins. Every time she thought of that, it stung. They hugged, hard, positive their unspoken thoughts were the same, just as Zack returned. "Okay, got that taken care of. Joe will be there at five."

Wait. Was he coming to the barbecue, too? *Boing* went her nerves.

See, this was the part about Lacy that sometimes aggravated her, pushing her to do things she wasn't ready to or comfortable with. Like forcing her mother to tell the truth or having to spend more time with Joe.

Had Eva been part of a setup? The anxiety bloomed as she realized that between Savannah, with her next rally plans, and Lacy and Zack, with whatever theirs were, she'd never be able to avoid the one man she had no business ever seeing again.

Chapter Five

For the first time since finding Lacy, Eva dragged her feet going to Zack's house for a visit. She'd taken Savannah home and afterward let Noah nap longer than usual because of all the excitement he'd had at the rally earlier in the day, missing his regular downtime. Of course, she wanted to spend time with her sister, but Joe would be there, and Joe made all kinds of confusing thoughts circle her brain.

Eva refused to be embarrassed about going after something she'd wanted in the heat of that moment, yet the consequence seemed to be regret. What about the mayor had caused her to act so out of character? And how, exactly, had she figured she'd never have to see him again? Obviously, thought hadn't played a part in her snap decision-making that night. Well, she was sane again now, and in the spirit of staying in that frame of mind, she'd continue to put her foot down on any future dealings with Joe.

Savannah would just have to find someone else to take her to the next rally.

So why did that plan feel all wrong?

Eva parked the car, gathered Noah and the over-size baby bag and then headed toward Zack's front porch, which wrapped around the entire structure. The house was painted a trendy gray with high-lighted beige and stone-colored river rock posts in front. Cherrywood double doors with stained glass sidelights covered nearly half of the front of the house. No wonder she'd hired him to do her remodel, the man was a construction wizard.

No sooner had she rung the bell than Zack rushed to open the door with one hand holding a platter of steaks. She must have caught him on a kitchen run. "Hey! We were getting worried something had happened to you." He looked at Noah and made a silly adult face in greeting. "Hi, buddy! Hungry?"

Noah squealed as he did regularly with Zack, which always made Eva wonder if the boy wanted and missed a man's company. Nah, he was so young, and she knew Mom was the most important person in his life and would be for years to come. Wasn't she?

"This guy overslept. Didn't have the heart to wake

him after all the excitement earlier." She closed the door and began to follow him.

"Grab a drink." He gestured toward the kitchen with his head. "I was just going to throw these on the grill."

Emma appeared from the back deck, rushing toward Noah. "Hi! Can I walk him?"

"Of course."

Noah loved hanging out with big kids in general, especially Emma. Fortunately, she loved hanging out with him, too. Eva took an orange-flavored sparkling water from the fridge and girded herself before making an appearance on the beautiful custom back porch deck. It paid to be a contractor when updating one's home, and Zack had gone all out to make the older house a welcoming family home. Lacy couldn't be luckier to have found a family man like him.

Lacy was happily in conversation with Joe, and it crossed Eva's mind how weird it might be for him to look at the identical twin of the woman he'd gone all the way with—as in all, *all* the way—in the back of a limousine. She shook her head to immediately erase the thought. Yet there he sat, with that thick black hair, workingman's shirt and those snug jeans and strong thighs—thighs she couldn't get out of her mind for days afterward—and Western boots. So very cowboy of him, not to mention entirely distracting.

"Hi!" Lacy jumped to her feet at the sight of her sister.

"Hiya." She opened her bottled drink for distraction while also trying her best to seem nonchalant as she nodded hello at Joe.

"Joe and I were just discussing the importance of being transparent when running for office."

Eva nearly spit out her first sip. Would Joe have the nerve to be *transparent* about them? She had to cover for her twisting gut and jangling nerves. "I don't think that Barnstable person got the memo. The whole fast food for cheaper breakfasts is so dishonest. Such a cover-up." She tried not to connect with his intelligent gaze.

"That's what I was saying," Joe said as he rose to greet her like a gentleman while a most ungentlemanly memory of where his hands had once been flashed before her.

She sucked a breath and couldn't very well ignore his outstretched offer for a shake. She took it, the immediate frisson traveling through her palm and up her arm as well as a few points south. "You should expose her."

This time she made the mistake of gazing into his eyes immediately after choosing an unfortunate word, *expose*, where a playful glint was unavoidable. "I plan to, as soon as possible."

Was that a double entendre message? Yeah, he'd exposed Eva the other night in quick order, too.

Completely. Such a naughty girl. *Wipe that secret lip twitch off your face, mister.* And there went the reflex blush. Which made her angry. A choice expletive popped into her brain. If she let it out, someone would have to cover Emma's and Noah's ears. So she took the snarky route and focused on the annoying Louella Barnstable. "She's probably been promised some kind of kickback."

"I don't like to make assumptions about people without hard facts," he retorted, shooting down her ungenerous comment.

"Anyway," Joe continued as he seemed to reluctantly let go of her hand. "Good to see you again, and thanks for bringing my future campaign mascot to the rally."

"You're welcome." Her first thought was that she hadn't had much choice, but she quickly remembered she was a grown woman and *always* had a choice. This one may not have been her best, though, and Lacy's invitation had really been an uncomfortable offer. Well, rather than clinch her buns all night, she may as well get on with an otherwise long and painful barbecue. The consequence of just once letting her hair down with a near stranger. "I noticed beer in the fridge," she asked the chef. "Okay if I grab one?"

"Of course," Zack said, busily arranging and re-arranging the meat on the grill. "Bring me one, too, please?" How could she refuse a guy in an apron?

"You got it." Then reluctantly she connected with Joe again. "Should I bring you one, too?"

His grateful nod flustered her, and she went on her way. Pull it together! He's a *politician*, remember?

After handing out the beers and popping the top on her own, she took a long, satisfying gulp and rounded on her sister, grabbed her by the arm and dragged her to the far side of the backyard.

"Was this a setup?" she stage-whispered.

Lacy made a noble attempt at looking innocent. "What? No! Zack wants to support Joe, that's all."

"And I needed to be here because?"

Lacy glanced at her ultra-white sneakers rather than Eva, then made a frustrated expression. "You're family? And I want to see you all the time?" she said, as though it hurt to have to remind Eva.

Immediately sad, Eva dialed back her tone, even though Lacy had a way of going overboard with everything, then acting hurt if Eva didn't sing along with the verse. It was one of the differences in how they'd been raised, and one they still needed to work on. Today wasn't the time to get into it, though."I understand, but you don't know the whole story about Joe."

"So tell me."

"Not here! And not ever without a bottle of wine and just the two of us."

The hurt look morphed into full attention mode.

"Okay. That sounds really intriguing and I don't know if I'll be able to wait."

"You'll *have* to." It was kind of fun dangling a meaty carrot and play-threatening her sister, but also sad to be reminded of all the years they'd missed out taunting each other and getting into arguments.

"So that leads me to the reason I asked you to come today."

What happened to *You're my sister and I just wanted to see you?* "See, I knew it was about him." She used her brows and a partial eye roll to indicate the handsome and disturbingly sexy man on the other side of the yard without looking in his direction. But Lacy turned and gave Joe a long gaze. So much for being discreet.

"No, actually, it isn't. It's about us."

Eva grabbed Lacy's arm and squeezed in anticipation. "Did you find something out about our adoption?"

Lacy shook her head, and Eva was immediately disappointed, but who was she to gripe when she'd yet to track down her own mother and grill her about it.

"I want to make a proposition that I hope you won't think is crazy."

Eva couldn't help but give Lacy, who always looked so darn earnest, especially right now, a big hug. "Nothing you could ever say or do would seem crazy to me. Unless it was trying to fix me up with a politician." No harm in setting limits, though.

"Okay, then, I'll just dive right in," Lacy said, ignoring the last phrase. "I want you and Noah to temporarily move in with me at Dad's house."

Eva couldn't help the reaction, her eyes widening and her chin tucking in.

"I know you're probably thinking why my house and not yours, the big, gorgeous and spacious house where all of Noah's stuff is. But I live here, in our dad's house, and we have thirty-one birthdays we missed out on sharing, and just as many Christmases. Before I marry Zack and start my life with him, I'd like to catch up on the ones we missed. As much as possible anyway. You and me and lots of birthday cake and sharing a room. If that's going too far, just tell me, and you can stay in the guest room."

Eva's heart melted with the idea even when her instinct put on the brakes. What if they drove each other nuts? And why was she the one who would have to pick up and move? "Stay in the guest room? What's wrong with me staying in my own house?"

"Shoot, I was worried I was asking too much, but this might be our only chance."

"Hold on, sis, we have the rest of our lives to get to know each other."

"But I'm talking about making up for the lost years."

"Is that even possible?"

"We won't know unless we try." There went that earnest lift of Lacy's brows and puppy dog eyes that could melt the hardest heart…like the aloof one that resided in Eva's chest.

"This is our one shot," Lacy made it sound as if one of them was going to prison. Typical for the way she liked to exaggerate. Of course Eva wanted to know her sister better, but the storybook way Lacy sometimes wanted to go about that journey wasn't at all Eva's more pragmatic style.

But Lacy was the one with a job to do right there in town with her food truck while Eva could work from her computer anywhere.

"To temporarily live together?"

Lacy nodded like a bobblehead.

"So of course it would be easiest for me and Noah to move in with you."

"Exactly. That way you can get to know our dad by living where he lived, and we can make up for lost time. You like the idea?"

Eva made a huge internal sigh realizing what she was up against. Lacy needed this for some reason, to help her transition to married life. Truth was, taking a break from her house during the bathroom re-model could be the perfect timing. And eating a lot of birthday cake didn't sound half bad, either. Only because the move would serve a purpose for both of them, Eva mentally let out her breath.

"I love it!" she said.

Later, they all sat on benches around the large custom-made table on the spacious wood deck, since summer still held on though it was approaching fall. Eva had made it a point to sit on the opposite side of Emma near Noah to ensure she wouldn't be in touching range of Joe or his thighs, or any part of him.

"This coleslaw is delicious," Joe said.

Emma sat up and preened as Lacy proudly looked on. "Our little future chef Emma made it."

"It was my idea to add the pineapple and peanuts. I saw it on the food channel."

"Outstanding," Joe continued. "May I have more?"

Sure it was sweet, but seriously, the comment was nothing short of "typical politician charming the crowd" stuff.

As Eva sat stewing in her negative thoughts, missing the moment to be gracious and hand the man the bowl, Emma reached over her, retrieved the serving dish and handed it across the table to the mayor.

Only then did Eva taste the coleslaw. "Man, this really is delicious."

"Thanks, Aunt Eva."

Wait. Yes, once Lacy married Zack, she *would* be an aunt. The changes in her life this past couple of months had been mind-boggling in a wonderful and terrific kind of way. Then, continuing on in her "wonderful" frame of mind, in a misguided move, she glanced at Joe.

"Can I bounce something off you guys?" Joe

asked while everyone dug into the great steak, salad and baked potato dinner. The garlic bread safely out of Noah's reach.

"Sure," Zack answered for the group. "And after, I've got some ideas to run by you, too."

"Okay. Well, here's the deal. First thing Monday morning I'm going to contact a few key businesses in town. The diner, a couple of cafés and Arnold's Family Restaurant on Main Street and ask them if they'd support a citywide senior discount for breakfast and lunch. First of all, what do you think? I hinted about it in the speech earlier. And second, is that asking too much of our small business owners?"

"Not at all," Lacy spoke first. "Not if it's voluntary. I've worked in the restaurant business for ten years and seniors are valued customers. Some may not leave big tips, but they like to eat out, often in large groups. Why not have early bird specials since so many seniors are early risers, and how about senior group lunch discounts, because they seem to like to go out to lunch with friends. Oh!" Lacy tapped the table as though struck by a sudden great idea. "I can park my truck in town a couple days a week specifically for breakfast sandwiches and charge half price for our senior citizens." Her big blue eyes went wider. "I can call the breakfast the Mayor McMuffin."

They all laughed about that.

"You could, but you could also get sued by Mc-

Donald's if you did," Joe said, putting on his lawyer hat.

"Ah, point taken. Maybe just Eggs in a Blanket, then? You know, because of the wrap."

Joe looked particularly tickled, and Eva realized the more time she spent around Joe the easier it was to react to him as a person, not only as a partner in passion. Unlike her preconceived ideas about *all* politicians, Joe was affable, low-key and, above all, sincere. Based on his speech earlier and his shared thoughts just now, he truly had a heart for his hometown and wanted to keep it a place where families would want to live and raise their kids. Well, that part, Eva kind of inferred, but it only made sense.

Truth was, she'd read up on him and discovered he also had an eye on the next generations, encouraging technology and millennial businesses, wanting to keep Generation Z around instead of having them head off to college never to return. She'd also noticed he was smart and considerate.

One other thought occurred. *Keep the people around, collect their taxes.* When had she turned into such a cynic?

But honestly, she had to stop adding to the list of his good traits because, as she'd made a severe point to him, on the personal level he would have to remain a one-time indulgence. Period. There simply was no point in letting herself like him as a person. She'd already ruined any chance of that after being skin to skin with him. It was impossible to begin at the grand finale and work backward.

As if that writing on the wall wasn't enough, she also had her long and abiding mistrust for men who came off as good guys. Like Lawrence had, in college. *Never again.* The overall truth was, she simply couldn't trust her instinct where men were concerned. Joe might seem one way around Lacy and Zack and the townspeople, but she had evidence he knew how to take what he wanted. Of course she'd offered herself on a platter. *Don't let that cloud your thinking.*

Eva's mind had busily wandered far away, and she'd obviously missed the rest of the dinner table conversation.

"I've got some news to share," Lacy said, brightening and sitting straighter. "Eva has agreed to move in with me right here in Little River Valley so we can make up for lost time before Zack and I get married."

Zack smiled and nodded, unsurprised. Lacy had obviously first run her plan by the man she loved. She was lucky to find a good guy like Zack, whereas Eva wasn't sure she'd know one if she saw him. That thought occurred at the exact moment she glanced at Joe Aguirre, who was also obviously happy for the sisters, and seeming maybe even a little too pleased?

At least she wouldn't have to see the guy again until his next rally at the high school. Or maybe she wouldn't have to see him again at all, if she found a ride replacement for Savannah. And yes, sad but true, she was doomed to be suspicious of all men's good intentions for the rest of her life, thanks to Lawrence.

Succinctly put, Joe was too good to be true.

Eva and Lacy didn't waste a second running back and forth on Sunday to Eva's house, and finally, in the late afternoon, Eva and Noah had moved into Lacy's house.

"You'll probably feel cramped here, but this guest bedroom is all I've got," Lacy said when they'd brought the last box of "essentials" for Eva into the small yellow room. Daisy, an old calico cat, reluctantly left her place on the foot of the bed when Lacy shooed her off. Lacy cast an apologetic glance as she wiped away cat fur that noticeably flew into the late-afternoon sunrays.

Never having owned a pet, Eva was determined to make things work for her sister and her big idea about making up for lost time. "I love it. Daisy can sleep in here whenever she wants, too. I'm the invader. And Noah even has his own room."

"Of sorts. The den, or alcove, or office space, yes. It was evidently good enough for me as a baby."

The quick thought of them being babies from the same womb and then ripped apart twisted at her chest. "Then it's good enough for Noah." Eva stopped puttering, making sure her sister understood how special their "making up time" would be. "The more I think about it, this is a great idea."

"You won't miss all your luxury?" Lacy asked, concern furrowing her brow.

"Not if you're around."

"Terrific." Lacy looked relieved but also distracted. "Now, while you finish up, I've got a birthday cake to bake."

Would they really celebrate thirty-one birthdays in two months? "Not wasting any time, I see." Eva worried about her future waistline.

"Nope. And this first one will be for ages one through five."

"Whew. Thank goodness we're doing them in batches. I was getting worried. Can't wait to see it."

"Noah's going to love it."

They laughed and hugged and already Eva knew she'd made the right decision. They might drive each other crazy in the end, but this would be their only chance to ever live together. Her big dream house could wait for the rest of her life. First, she had catching up to do.

In the half year since she'd moved to Santa Barbara, she'd already figured out that the size of a residence didn't make it a home. She'd grown up in a huge house that had always felt empty and lonely. It was the sense of belonging that made a person feel whole and part of a family, which was something she'd always felt lacking, except for when Nana was around. She understood her mother loved her, but she was single and had to work hard for her living, which meant loads of time away from that enormous house. Someone had to pay for it. She knew she could find that sense of belonging with Lacy and Noah, and that was more than enough to ask of any house, big or small.

After Eva put the last of her suitcase of clothes in the drawers, Lacy stepped back into the room, and Eva took the opportunity to ask what was on her mind. "So what's that one more thing you wanted to tell me?"

"Oh, uh, well, now that you're moved in and everything, and isn't it great to be living together? Like we should've all our lives?"

"Yes, I admit it. These next weeks will be fun." But she was also getting a teeny-tiny bit suspicious about Lacy's overly rah-rah approach. Even for Lacy, it seemed over the top.

"Good." Lacy only fiddled with her hands when she was nervous, which she did now, lacing, unlacing fingers, rubbing her knuckles. "So what I needed to tell you was that, uh, well, I'll just spit it out. Joe Aguirre is my neighbor."

Eva's stomach nose-dived to her knees. Had she heard right?

"He lives two houses down."

Two houses! "What?"

Lacy had a cagey expression, and for the first

time, unnerved, Eva was disappointed in her sister. "This was all a trick?" If it was, they were on the verge of having their first major argument.

"Nooo. No. I promise you no. I wanted you to move in, but I noticed you seem to have this love-hate thing with Joe, so I was hesitant."

"Not love *or* hate!" They had nothing going on except for one night filled with crazy, hot sex.

"No, those are strong words. But let's just say you tend to overreact regarding anything that has to do with him, and I don't understand why."

Had Eva been that obvious? Did everyone else pick up on that, too? She kept her mouth shut, not wanting to give anything away.

"So I was afraid you wouldn't want to move in if I told you he lived there." Lacy pointed to the right side of the house.

"I can't believe you did this!"

Lacy looked distressed by Eva's accusations, but Eva couldn't help believing her sister's intentions had been sincere. "Would you believe, I did it because I love you?"

"Ugh!" Eva grabbed her head, a sudden ache cutting down the center. "How am I supposed to avoid him now?"

Lacy glanced to the floor and back up, half her mouth hitched upward, her gaze asking for mercy. "I don't think you should."

"Don't get any ideas," Eva warned.

"Got it. And remember he's a busy man. You'll probably never run into him. I hardly ever do. He's got a city to run and a campaign to win."

The promise was not exactly comforting, but Eva wasn't about to pack up and move back home over it. Lacy came first. The mayor, well, he was another story.

"Oh, and our cake's ready. Let's go sing 'Happy Birthday.'"

Eva sighed, then smiled. They were really doing this.

The next day, Lacy had already left for her early-morning food truck stops when Eva woke and decided to jump right into her normal routine, which meant a morning jog. The sisters had stayed up late, sharing as much as they could remember from the first five years of their separated childhoods, especially birthdays and Christmases.

Eva rushed out the front door and turned left at the street, in the opposite direction of where Lacy had pointed out Joe lived. With Noah happily waiting for his morning run, she pushed the high-end jogging stroller and started at a slow pace to help warm up. At the first corner turn, she slammed on the brakes, nearly flipping Noah out of the stroller. Ten feet away, there was Joe, obviously at the end of his jog. His T-shirt was off and getting used as a rag to wipe the sweat from his face. Oh yeah, she remembered those muscular shoulders and chest, not to mention the trim torso and abs. He wore sports shorts that accentuated those amazing thighs, and footies with high-end name-brand running shoes she'd expected to see him wearing at the rally on Saturday, not those boots. Man, he had defined calves, too. *Look away. Look away!*

"Eva?" he seemed as surprised as she was to literally run into her. And he knew it was her, not Lacy. Interesting. Of course, Noah and the stroller was probably a huge giveaway. Unlike Joe, who was nearly naked, she was three-quarters covered in yoga wear, though everything fit like a second skin to her body. There was no hiding, and he noticed.

"Oh, hi," she said, as if they met up like this every morning.

He stopped cold. "Lacy didn't tell you we were neighbors, did she?"

"Not until I'd unpacked and made myself at home."

He bent and peeked at Noah, who was still raring to go and showing signs of impatience. He'd thrown his rubber rattle on the sidewalk, or maybe it'd toppled out when Eva had almost launched him into space. Joe picked it up and handed it back to him, before returning his gaze to Eva as he straightened up, his eyes scraping along every inch of her. "Look, I'm sorry to put you in this awkward situation."

"Well, it may be a little inconvenient, but we can

always avoid each other. Anyway, it's more important that Lacy and I spend time together and work on our crazy adoption arrangements. Can you believe that grown-ups would come up with such a horrible plan to separate twins?"

"Only in a movie." He shook his head in solidarity of thought.

Wait, a movie? Ah, *The Parent Trap*. Had they gotten the idea from there?

"If you ever need a lawyer to help dig into your birth records, I'd have better access, just let me know. I'd be happy to help."

See, this was why she couldn't write the guy off as easily as she thought. Every chance he had, he said or did something that qualified him as a considerate, nice person. "Well, thank you. We'll let you know."

"And for the record," he said, glancing right and left before saying his next thought, "I don't know what came over me that night." He said in a lowered voice.

"You can't take all the blame. I was right there with you." Embarrassed about meeting in broad daylight, alone together for the first time since their night of passion, admitting what they'd done, she was jarred back to her forgotten adolescence. "They must have put something in that champagne." Sure, blame it on a mysterious outside force. How mature.

He laughed, most likely out of courtesy. "I'm positive we both knew what we were doing."

He certainly had! Wow. Great lover. *And here comes the blush*. Noah fussed, drawing her back to the moment. She bent to make sure he was all right, handing the rubber rattle back to him for the second time. "You're right. We're just going to have to deal with it like adults."

"Agreed."

"So quit checking out my butt."

He cleared his throat. Guilty as charged. "My apologies for putting you in a tough spot, especially with your sister wanting you to move in and all."

"What about you? You're the one running for mayor." He didn't corner the market on consideration, she could be nice, too. Maybe it was time to show him.

He sighed. "Like I said, I don't know what came over me that night."

They took a moment to look into each other's eyes—she had to pull her gaze from his bare chest to do it—and sure enough, even at seven in the morning there were bedroom sparks arcing between them. She needed to run for the hills or risk making another mistake. Thank her lucky stars she had Noah with her this time.

"One other thing," he said breaking the brief though intense silence.

She watched and waited, fully aware of his post-run scent and shaken by her visceral response.

"I was wondering if we could start over."

Not at all what she expected to hear. He was supposed to do the gentlemanly thing and steer clear. Not start over! "I made it clear I had no intention of ever..."

"That's not what I'm talking about." His knuckles sat low on his hips as he stood in a wide-legged stance, looking so annoyingly athletic. "I'd like to start at square one and get to *know* you. That's all."

"What would be the point?" she said, baffled by his illogical suggestion.

"We could be friends?"

"Not after *that* start." She pointed behind with her thumb as though their night together followed in a looming gray cloud.

"Have lunch with me."

"Oh no." She straightened her posture in opposition, pointing him out. "You're reeling me in. Oh, just a harmless lunch. Like that harmless Dreams Come True dinner."

Her insinuation registered in his dark brown gaze.

"No way," she added.

"You have my word it won't happen again." Spoken like a true politician.

She couldn't believe him, yet something about his body language and authentic tone said otherwise. What should she do?

"Have lunch with me. There are at least three cafés in the town center that serve alfresco. We'd be out in the open, just talking like regular folks. Starting at square one."

"Why?"

His sincere expression turned to solemn. "Because I like you? And I'd like to know you better."

She couldn't help the adolescent scoff. "I think we already covered that part."

"Let's start fresh. Take one step at a time. Lunch? Today at one?"

Was she really going along with his crazy idea to pretend their time in that limousine had never happened? Could they possibly pull that off, and handle the simple act of getting to know each other? Or was he pulling a Lawrence? Some kind of bet or scam. Maybe with Mike? A tiny voice said, *Take a chance. Find out. You can always walk away. You're in charge of your life.* By this point the tiny voice was yelling. *Say no or yes but say something.* "Okay. Where?"

"Grace's? You know the place?"

"I'll find it." Resigned, yet, if she was honest, with a spark of excitement.

They stood for another moment as Joe shared his earnest and obviously pleased smile, when a car turned the corner and slowed down. "Mayor Aguirre?" someone said from inside.

Eva looked in the direction of the voice at the exact moment a flash went off from a cell phone, which made it impossible to see who it was. Just like Saturday at the rally, though with a much better camera there, some photographer was working overtime. Would the local newspaper track down a man on his morning jog?

"Hey!" Joe yelled as the car sped off. "I'm going to have to add that to my to-do list this morning. Call the *Voice* and get to the bottom of this."

"What if it's not them but someone hired by Louella Barnstable?" Leave it to Eva to think the worst of a politician. "This could turn out to be a social media campaign, which is farther reaching than a small-town newspaper these days. Sadly."

"Like a smear tactic?"

"What else?" Because who played fair in politics these days?

Joe's prior sweet and flirtatious overtones dissipated as his face paled at the suggestion.

"Maybe we shouldn't meet for lunch," she said, sensing a way out and grabbing it.

He shook his head. "Once you get to know me better, you'll realize how wrong that suggestion was. I'll be at Grace's at one. Hope to see you there, where we'll eat in public and enjoy ourselves, whether my opponent likes it or not."

Just what Eva needed, some fake scandal to cover up their real scandal.

Fear crept through Eva's every nerve. Those tinted sliding windows between the driver and the rest of the limousine really were impossible to see through, right? The driver couldn't hear over the music pumping through the speakers, could he?

She left Joe on the sidewalk, pushing on with her jog, needing more than ever to take a run. To run from him. To think. The instant she got home she'd look at the contract with the limousine company and especially the clause about the driver and occupant privacy.

The last thing she wanted to do was ruin someone's career because of an impulse. Especially her own.

Chapter Six

"**Y**ou gotta see this, man," Mike said later that morning at Joe's office, handing him the local newspaper.

Joe dreaded what he might see but reminded himself the incident with the car had only occurred a couple of hours ago. And really, what had they seen except for two adults talking in broad daylight with a kid in the stroller between them. Completely innocent stuff.

"It's not the front page, but page two is good," Mike continued.

Joe liked the photo of him onstage at the Oakland Bowl, talking to the crowd. They'd caught him in a good light as he made a point with a typical politician's hand gesture. Being a lawyer, arguing cases, had been great preparation. Savannah smiled in the background and—uh-oh, the folly of his having Eva join them onstage became clear—Eva was also smiling with little Noah on her hip.

It hadn't occurred to him before. The kid with midnight hair and olive skin looked far more like Joe than the fair-skinned redhead. What might Louella make of that? Just what he needed, someone whispering love-child accusations, because the truth had a way of getting buried in the lead. Most people never made it past the headline.

With trepidation he perused the article and was relieved. Though paraphrased, the gist of his speech had been reported without his ideas being twisted. True, there were an equal number of the senior protesters' pictures on page three, but who could resist a group of senior citizens picketing at a political gathering? It was so 1960s, like back in their heyday. He only wished Louella hadn't registered so prominently in most of those photos.

"Not bad," he concluded.

"Agreed. Now what?"

"I'm about to make cold calls to several businesses asking if they would consider giving breakfast discounts to people over sixty."

"Sounds good. And after that?"

Why did it always feel like a press conference

with Mike since he became his campaign manager? "I do have a city to run and meetings to attend."

"And after that?"

"I'm having lunch." It was the first thing Joe said that sparked interest from Mike.

"A photo op lunch?"

Joe soundly shook his head no. "Hands off this one."

Mike gave his signature skeptical raise of the brow.

"I mean it. Whatever I do with Eva DeLongpre from here on out is off the record. Got it?"

Mike took a couple of seconds to digest the inference of what he'd just heard. "Yes, jefe."

Having found a parking spot in front, Eva arrived at the Grace's Café entrance at the Main Street Outdoor Mall nervous beyond explanation—because, seriously, wasn't it the "will we, won't we" question that made dating someone anxiety-producing?

"I'm meeting someone for lunch on the patio," she said, smoothing the pale floral-patterned thigh-length cardi sweater over her denim leggings, adjusting the large blue-and-beige beads of her long necklace over the white top beneath.

"Right this way," the young woman said, seeming to know exactly where to seat Eva.

She took this chance to flounce her hair and fluff it out. Why was she so nervous?

Thankfully, Lacy was done with her morning roadside service and didn't work the lunch crowd on the days she ran the food truck. She'd been more than happy to watch Noah, and then overjoyed—thrilled was more like it—when Eva told her who the lunch date was with.

Joe stood as Eva approached, pushing out the wrought iron chair frame with the back of his knees and causing loud scraping on the brick patio. His handsome smile briefly stopped the breath in her throat. He stretched to pull out her chair before the hostess could.

"Right on time," he said, with obvious approval.

"Can't very well keep the mayor waiting, can I?"

He sat after she did, and after the menus were handed out and the young woman left, he immediately put his down. "Let's leave that mayor business behind. Okay? Right now, it's just you and me."

Which was why she was nervous. Because of what had happened the last time they were completely alone. She glanced around the outdoor setting. Trees everywhere, birds chirping, the sky blue and the temperature Southern California normal. Eternal spring. Not to mention the smell of fresh baked bread in the air. Perfectly safe.

"Ready for lunch—" he picked up his menu "—on a beautiful September day." He began perusing it.

She inhaled a large portion of the fresh air and mentally rolled her shoulders. Joe was a nice guy, not to mention easy on the eyes; why not relax and enjoy herself. If his plan was to start from scratch and work their way to where they'd left off the first night they'd met, they had a lot of catching up to do. Who knew, it might even be fun. But she had zero intention of ever letting whatever *this* was he was going for get *that* far again.

"I'm curious about the senior breakfast discounts." Her plan was to keep this luncheon extremely superficial.

"My calls and visits went great. Half a dozen places are willing to give substantial daily discounts for the local seniors. Or at least try it out. A couple others agreed to make the deal one day a week. I plan to make more calls and visits tomorrow farther out from the business district."

"That's great. Your city seems very supportive of you."

"I'm supportive of my small business owners."

As in—you scratch my back and I'll scratch yours? She hoped that wasn't the routine. Something told her that wouldn't be the case with Joe.

She shook off the memory of Lawrence, the opportunist who'd turned her into such a doubter where men were concerned. It might take a lifetime to get over the humiliation he'd caused. But Joe clearly wasn't Lawrence, so on this beautiful day she would cut him some slack. Joe was a man who had good relationships with the local business owners and their respect was mutual. Period.

After they made their orders and their drinks were delivered—both got iced tea: hers sweetened, his not—he finally gave her a long, silent study.

"You look very nice today, like you always do." There was nothing but sincerity in his gaze.

"Thank you. You do, too." She also played it honest.

Half his mouth tilted upward. "Can we get any *more* formal?"

"I know." With his naming their problem, she relaxed. "How do you want to work this?"

"Okay, I'll start," he said when a basket of that great smelling rosemary and olive oil bread got delivered to the table along with their salads. "I read your bio on the Dreams Come True website before the big dinner, and though I was impressed with your résumé, I was taken by surprise when I met you."

"Surprised?" She ripped her roll in half and lathered it with a small pat of butter that had a tiny, edible lavender blossom on it.

"I fully expected an unapproachable, wealthy and snooty society type."

"Well, thanks a lot." The only person who'd ever described her that way had been Lawrence, on the day he'd demeaned himself and her in public. She tensed, holding off on taking a bite of bread. He noticed.

"And you turned out to be the exact opposite." He

also took some bread, broke it, leaving half on the small plate and skipping the butter. "I hope my expectations didn't offend you. I'm just being honest, and hope you'll do the same."

Most people didn't hold such stereotypical views on privilege without some sort of personal experience. It made her wonder who'd done what to Joe. Her research on him suggested he was an overachiever, which made her wonder if it came naturally or if he had something to prove.

"In that case, I admit I read your bio on the internet, too. Also quite impressive. You've proved a lot over the years." Now she gobbled her first delicious bite. Where would the world be without yeast, herbs and butter?

"*Prove*. That's an interesting choice of word." He studied her as she enjoyed the roll. "Makes it sound like I needed to."

She'd unintentionally touched a tender spot of his personality, so why not be blunt. "Do you?"

To that, she got a long, thoughtful and unreadable stare as he took a bite of his salad and mulled over her challenge.

"Overachievers and all, that's who I'm referring to." She dug into her leafy greens, loaded with fresh and most likely local veggies and homemade salad dressing. "They usually have something to prove."

"My parents worked hard to give me a foot up and I felt obliged to make the best use of it. They taught

me that hard work was the key. What I discovered
was sometimes hard work and achievements still
didn't make the grade for some people."

She suddenly understood where this conversation was going. "As in *still* not being good enough?"

"You're very astute for a rich girl." She didn't
mind his gentle slur.

Okay. Things were getting honest. She would normally bristle being called out, but they were onto
something, with him not feeling good enough and
her always having to make people look beyond the
obvious with her wealth. "And rich girls aren't supposed to be intuitive?" She knew the drill; it was
easy to label "types."

"Not in my experience, but *you* are different."

His was a prickly response, which made her wonder who'd mistreated him. "Some rich babe curve
you?" It didn't feel right using slang on him, but it
seemed one step removed this way, in case she'd hit
the nail.

Yikes. Right between the eyes. From the muscles
knotting at his jaws, the man still carried a grudge.
"I was willing to try. She wasn't. Small-town law-
yers aren't big on the society marriage list."

Which explained why his bio said "single" without further explanation on his social media page.
Keep it light, the man had obviously been hurt once
upon a time. "Am I supposed to have a marriage list?

Never knew. I've been too busy working on the non-profit and raising my son."

"Like I said, you seem different."

She ate a few bites and let that sink in, his insistence that she was different. Did he know, or was he just hoping? "For the record, I know what it's like."

Their meals were delivered, and it seemed like a good time to focus on the food instead of sharing more than they cared to right off. It was probably another side effect of sleeping with someone first, then deciding to get to know them. Though, throughout the mostly quiet meal, they caught each other's gaze and smiled or nodded before commenting how good the food was. Harmless, safe conversation. Still, it seemed they'd reached an understanding. They'd both been stung by at least one past relationship.

"So tell me about your childhood," Eva said when nearly half her lunch was eaten. "Where were you raised?"

"Right here in Ventura County. My parents worked the farms. Dad worked his way up to foreman and Mom trained to be a mortician."

Eva jerked her head up. "A mortician?"

"Unofficial training and education, never got a certificate, but it was a huge step up from breaking her back picking strawberries. She still works at the Perez Family Mortuary. Anyway, they made a good life for me. As you can see, my roots are humble."

"And impressive. You're a lawyer and the mayor. They must be thrilled."

Typical humble Joe, he merely took another bite of lunch rather than gloat.

"Were they at the rally Saturday?"

He shook his head. "All they know is hard work. There was a funeral, and it's moving toward harvest season at the avocado and almond farm. Which means both of them are working six days a week. Taking off to see their son give a speech isn't high on their list."

Eva's heart clutched hearing about this side of Joe. "When you get elected, they'll come to the party?"

Joe smiled at her positive assumption, and she was quickly reminded how taken she was by him physically. "Absolutely. As long as it's after work hours."

"They sound inspiring."

"They taught me a solid work ethic."

She had to give her mother credit for also teaching her about work ethic. While Eva had been so busy criticizing her mom for not being around, Bridget DeLongpre had worked her butt off providing that extra large house and all the goodies that went along with it. A sudden urge to contact her mom, which didn't occur often, swelled in her heart. "My mom did, too."

"So there, we've got something in common."

She put her napkin on the nearly empty plate and slid it away, smiling sincerely. "I suppose we do."

"Step one," he said.

"Easy-peasy." Her first notion was to put a halt to going any further, but she'd enjoyed his company. The man was solid and down-to-earth, like her sister Lacy. Good qualities in a human being. And also in a man, regardless of where and how he grew up.

"Let's take a walk. I know a little place that makes the best churros in Ventura."

"Sounds great, but I'm full, and I can't stick Lacy with watching Noah all afternoon after working this morning. Besides, don't you have a city to run?"

"I do, but this place isn't far." He stopped, seeming to mentally take a step back. "Look, I understand. We'll get one next time."

Next time?

"How about dinner tomorrow night?"

She shook her head. He was moving way too fast. Oh, wait, they'd already done that. Okay, so he was trying to catch up, but did they need to rush things? "Is it okay if I think about it?"

"Absolutely. Let me give you my number. You call when you're ready for dinner."

For a change, she didn't intimidate a man on the silly grounds of being rich.

Eva had done her share of dating, but she'd never experienced a man so confident and straightforward. He was obviously used to running the show, and she admitted she kind of liked him taking charge. Which, as she recalled, he'd gladly done the other night, once she'd started things off.

She didn't want to end the lunch date on a full-blown blush, but it was too late.

"Okay" was all she said.

Then he walked her to her car, where she was taken by surprise over being disappointed Joe hadn't tried to kiss her. But then it was broad daylight on Main Street in Little River Valley, and he was the mayor. Surely he'd calculated what kind of impression that would make on the voting public.

Eva was grateful, too, because that was the last thing she wanted to do—get closer to him.

Joe arrived at the mayor's office in plenty of time to prepare for the City Council meeting set for 2:00 p.m. Today's topic, city budget and building permits. They were a council divided on the building permits, some agreeing with Louella. He bookmarked the file on his laptop, closed it and tucked it under his arm, then prepared to head across the quad for city hall when Mike rushed into his office. He looked flushed, as if he'd run from the parking lot and maybe taken the stairs rather than wait for the old and slow elevator in the two-story building. Something he never did.

"Not good," Mike said. "This is a nightmare."

Joe furrowed his brow, watched and waited for Mike to bring up something on his cell phone. "I just got a Google alert about you and you won't believe what's circulating around the internet."

The great lunch he'd just enjoyed with Eva soured in his stomach. On Mike's phone, there was an image of Joe and Eva, in their jogging clothes, talking. The picture must have been taken prior to the one that had been clicked when the car stopped by them. From this angle it appeared that they were flirting. There was no other way to describe the goofy grins on their faces.

The caption read, "Is Mayor Aguirre hiding a family?"

Next to that picture was a snapshot from the rally on Saturday, but this one zeroed in on Eva holding Noah on her hip. She smiled supportively in the background as Joe gave his speech.

The caption under that one asked, "Does the mayor have a love child?"

His exact words!

He went on to read from the accompanying report.

For a politician who preaches transparency, our mayor seems to have some questions to answer.

The Facebook page was called the Little River Valley Beat by a Kitty Mittens, Feline at Large.

Irate, he lashed out. "I can't let a stupid gossip column influence my campaign."

"The FB page has a couple thousand followers," Mike was quick to point out.

"Those followers could be from all over the country. Most of them probably don't even vote."

"True. But stuff like this can go viral."

"We weren't flirting, we were talking. We accidentally ran into each other."

"That picture says otherwise."

Joe looked again at the photo and had to admit they looked like they were enjoying their talk. The interchange looking downright intimate.Then another post popped up. With a picture. One that couldn't be brushed off as accidental. Their luncheon date.

Not that a mayor wasn't allowed to date, but these pictures implied he was hiding something, like a child and possibly a woman. He'd been mayor for the last several years, which people could construe as a quiet scandal happening on his watch.

Why was he even thinking this way? It was craziness, and he couldn't buy into this gossip's insinuations.

"Find out who this Kitty Mittens is. I'll set whoever it is straight face-to-face," he said on his way out the door, heading for his meeting, thoughts scattered thanks to anger.

"I'm on it," Mike called out as he took his first look at the newest post. *"¿Estás bromeando?"*

"What? What's a joke?"

Mike shared the post.

Starting to feel paranoid, Joe realized someone

had seen his luncheon date today. Where had they been sitting? Was it the hostess or server? His first thought was to be grateful Eva hadn't agreed to dinner tomorrow night, because he'd hate to have to break it. His second thought was, *I'm not letting that stupid Facebook page interfere with my personal life.*

He had nothing to hide.

The image of a stretch limousine appeared in his thoughts. Oh yes, he did.

His third thought was—*I've got a right to a private life. If I want to date Eva, nothing is going to stop me.*

Later, after Noah had gone down for the night, Eva and Lacy stood in the small, old-fashioned kitchen, opting to talk instead of watch TV. Lacy had grilled Eva about the luncheon date during dinner.

"It sounds like you had a really nice time today. Why didn't you accept his dinner offer?"

Now Eva grew antsy. "It's too soon. He seems too..." She couldn't even formulate her thoughts, wanting to resist his appeal by keeping everything blurry.

"He's a busy man. He's the mayor and has a law practice." Lacy took a couple glasses from the cabinet. "He doesn't have time to spare, you know? Yet he asked you to dinner. That's a major compliment."

"I get it, but..."

Lacy took the handle of the refrigerator, then

stopped. "It seems more like you just want to keep Joe at arm's length."

Eva fiddled with her fingers and stared out the window. "Yeah, well, I don't trust men much. Especially the ones I find attractive."

"I knew you thought he was good-looking!" Lacy pointed as though Eva had just been accused of a crime in the courtroom. "Couldn't help but notice, like every time you look at him!" She finally opened the refrigerator and took out a bottle of white wine. "It's obvious he's attracted to you, too, so why not find out where things could go?"

She already knew—straight to bed. A place neither of them needed to be at this time in their lives. Eva ground her teeth and stared at her shoes. Old, painful memories returning against her will. "It's a long story."

"And I've got all the time in the world." Lacy handed Eva a glass of wine and led her to the comfortable living room in the house she'd grown up in, helped her sister sit and then joined her on the comfy but broken-in couch.

After a few moments of contemplation, then a quick sip of the fruity wine, Eva swallowed her pride and decided to share a story she hadn't told anyone since the day it'd happened. "I'd just finished my master's in business at Pepperdine, with the world at my fingers. At least that's how it should've been. Instead, all I felt was heartbreak." She shook her head at the horrible memories, took another sip of wine as fortification and, for the sake of her sister, ploughed on. "Between my yearning for closeness all my life. You know how that feels."

"Exactly."

"And being naive enough to be a dreamer, I fell in with a guy who wound up ripping out my heart in the worst possible way." She sipped more while seeing how deeply Lacy was touched by her words. How wonderful it was to share with her sister, even though the memories were awful, and she never wanted to bring them up again. Yet, for Lacy, she would be brutally honest.

"I thought this guy who came out of nowhere was my fate. Turned out one of Lawrence's stupidly rich friends had dared him to make a date with 'the rich and stuck-up redhead,' which was the *only* reason he'd invited me to go out that first time."

"Bastard!"

"I know, right? Still, we dated for a while and I was positive he really liked me. He said he did anyway. He wasn't rich, by the way. Just liked to hang out with folks who had money, I guess. So apparently the dares escalated, and so did the payoffs, and, long story short, he took me to bed. I thought we had something special. I found out later he'd gotten another two hundred dollars for that."

The awful memory, and how it'd made her feel cheap and dirty, returned.

Lacy inhaled, shocked by the rottenness of what Eva had just shared. "He used you?"

"In the most humiliating kind of way." She took another sip of the wine, as did Lacy, during a short silence. "Yeah, so all that time I'd started thinking I don't care about Lawrence not coming from money, he's the one for me. Sleeping with him made me think I loved him. And he was a damn good actor. I only found out about their rotten *deals* when I overheard Harrison, the guy who was paying him, make the last and biggest dare of all for Lawrence. For three times as much money."

"What kind of sick person does that?"

"I'm still trying to figure that out." Eva shrugged, realizing she'd probably be baffled until the day she died.

"I'm not sure I want to hear this," Lacy said. "Not without more wine. Hold on."

Back in a jiffy, bringing the bottle then topping off both of their glasses, Lacy squeezed Eva's arm and looked empathetically into her eyes. "I wish I could've been there for you."

"I'm not sure even you could've helped with this."

"What did he bet?"

"Harrison wanted to see Lawrence break up with me. In public. He wanted to see a big dramatic scene where everyone would stop what they were doing and watch me get what was coming to me."

"And that a-hole Lawrence agreed?"

Eva nodded, tears welling in her eyes. She swatted them away, angry she still cared. But retelling the story made it real again, as though it had just happened last week. "He cared about the money more than me. And I eventually found out that all Harrison wanted to do was get back at me for turning him down for a date the year before. I didn't even remember it! The guy's ego was that wimpy."

"Evil, more like it."

"He was probably horrible at sex, too."

"Probably couldn't get it up." Lacy upped the ante on insults, much to Eva's appreciation. "It's a good thing I don't own a shotgun and I can't travel back in time."

That got a half-hearted reaction from Eva, a sad attempt at a courtesy laugh. How different would her life have been if she'd had Lacy in her corner from day one? "He was rich and thought he could do whatever he wanted, and Lawrence didn't have a cent and let the extra cash flow define his character."

Lacy moved in for a hug and Eva forced her tears to stop. No way was she going to give those two losers another second of having power over her. She sniffed hard, finished the last of the wine in her glass. "Anyway, I was never more hurt or furious in my life, but the hurt turned out to be stronger. I was so heartbroken and sad. Mom took me on a European vacation to help me forget."

"Wow."

Eva laughed with embarrassment. "I know, she thought she could buy my happiness. I was never more miserable while seeing the most amazing places in my life. And it took a long time to forget how Lawrence threw me to the curb for cash. It's left a permanent mark on my heart, Lacy. Rich guys. Poor guys. Neither can be trusted. Especially the men who seem too good to be true. I've dated a lot since then. At first, I didn't take anyone seriously, just kept things superficial. When a guy wanted to get serious, I'd think up an excuse. Then I'd meet someone I really liked but never let myself get comfortable around them. Sometimes I think I'm incapable of letting my guard down. I just keep waiting for something bad to happen.

"I dated one man for half a year just before I decided to adopt Noah. I was honest with him about my intentions, and he said he was fine with it…until I actually went through with the adoption. Then when most of my time and energy was directed toward my son, he just kind of drifted away. Since then, I haven't even bothered to think about men.

"So, no matter how great you and Zack insist Joe is, I'd have to get over thinking he's not interested in me for me. That it's either for my money or my connections. For what he can get out of it. Never just me."

Lacy put down her glass and scooted closer to

Eva, pulling her in for a tight hug. "My dear, dear sister, we've got to get you over that lie."

Old, ugly defeat spread from the tip of Eva's head to the ends of her toes. Wasn't it about time to let go of those old negative feelings? "I really am sick of thinking this way, Lacy. And I sure can use your help, because seeing you and Zack together gives me hope."

Chapter Seven

After another round of cheerleading from Lacy about what a great guy Joe Aguirre was, Eva and her sister said good-night. She checked on Noah, who was snuggled comfortably in his portable crib, covered him again with a light blanket and then got ready for bed.

When she pulled the covers over her, without a thought she reached for her cell phone. After a quick scroll through her emails she noticed a text from a couple of hours ago.

Had a great time at lunch today. J.

It was nearly eleven, but being mayor, he was

LYNNE MARSHALL 139

probably still up doing something work related or campaign planning, so she replied simply: Me, too.

Lacy's unwavering support of Joe's character had impressed her, forcing her to take a second look, and while still mildly under the influence of a great pinot grigio, she wrote one more text. Still want to have dinner?

Within seconds her phone rang, sending a thrill right through the sheets. It was Joe.

"Sometimes texts don't come off right," he said. "I'd love to have dinner with you but, if you don't mind, would prefer we had it at my house."

What? "Uh, that didn't even come off right over the phone." Talk about a come-on. "I was adamant we weren't going that route again." And honestly, she was disappointed he wanted to, though she could understand why…firsthand. His suggestion of starting at the beginning and getting to know each other was sweet, but was it just a cheap advance?

"That's not at all what I mean. Here's the thing. Some pictures of us from this morning have surfaced on a Facebook page. I think we should stay out of public together."

"All we were doing was talking!"

"That's what I thought, too. Until I saw the picture."

"What do you mean? Did they doctor them?"

"No." He went quiet a second, as if thinking of the best way to say something. "We look like two people who really like each other. Like we know each other really well."

Eva's cheeks warmed. They couldn't deny what was there between them and someone had caught it on camera. Great. "I'm not sure how to respond to that." Just great.

"Own it?" Even on the phone she could tell he was smiling, goading her to accept what they already both knew. "It wasn't like I was leering or anything, and you, well, you didn't exactly look coy."

"Can you forward it to me?"

Bing! And there it was. Evidence. Any person on the street could tell they really liked each other. They had more than a one-night fling going on. Or, from the picture, were going to be intimate again soon. How was that possible?

"Okay," she said. "We'll skip that dinner."

"That's the last thing I want to do. And why I suggested eating in at my house."

The part of her that liked to be in control, especially when she felt vulnerable, took charge. "How about next Wednesday night, here at Lacy's?"

"A whole week?"

"You said we needed to cool it. I'm offering a date. Take it or leave it."

She'd quickly learned that Wednesday night was Lacy's sleepover at Zack's. She also sensed she'd be less willing to have a repeat performance with Joe under the roof of the father she'd never met. Especially giving herself another week to cool off. Lop-sided logic, but it worked for her.

"Okay. If that's what you want. Sounds good."

He didn't even put up a fight, just accepted her need to distance their time together. What kind of man did that? A good man. "All right, then. See you next Wednesday. How about seven thirty so Noah will be in bed."

"It's a plan. Something to look forward to."

Liking the way that sounded a little too much, Eva made it a point to rein in any expectations. "*Just* dinner."

"Got it. Can we also have conversation?"

Joe was being understanding in a teasing way, but she liked that about him, and it made her want to play back. "We'll discuss that when you co—" she quickly corrected the word that could be considered a double entendre "—uh, get here."

He laughed lightly, obviously onto her, which made her smile in the dark. "Good night, Eva."

"Good night, Joe."

"Looking forward to a week from Wednesday."

She kicked off the covers, which suddenly felt far too warm.

"What are you going to cook?" Lacy asked the following Monday in the kitchen, after Eva finally admitted to the follow-up date. Lacy seemed as excited about the date as Eva, if not more.

Though Eva admitted she was holding back. Not wanting to let on how charged she was about the date, she casually poured herself a cup of coffee. "I'll order in."

"Why not cook for him?" Lacy leaned against the counter, arms crossed over her chenille bathrobe.

"You're the one who inherited that gene, not me." She opened the refrigerator and took out some creamer, focusing all her attention on the task so as to avoid Lacy's gaze.

"I can teach you." Lacy handed her the sponge to clean where the cream missed the cup as Eva poured.

"Not interested." She finally made eye contact. "I'll order from the Local Grown Restaurant."

"No, you won't. I used to work there. I can make you something better than that."

"It's your night at Zack's!"

"I can make enough for all of us and leave half with you."

Eva was a businessperson who knew a good deal when she heard one. Why argue?

By Wednesday afternoon, jitters started to saturate Eva's mood about the dinner date. Within a few hours she'd be alone in the house with Joe. Thankfully, Noah would be here, but he'd be asleep by then. The thing that jangled her nerves more than being alone with Joe again was looking forward to it. Was it possible for this one politician to break the mold from all the others? She had it on Lacy's word that was a fact. The good-guy politician. How often over the years had she seen that claim go up in flames?

Regardless, she admitted she liked what she'd experienced of him as a person, and she'd agreed to have dinner with him. Inside. Not in public. Because apparently, they were already an item.

She'd gone casual since they were eating in. She'd chosen a navy blue cashmere-infused cable-knit sweater, fashioned with a hoodie and side slits for style, over beige cotton herringbone gauze pants with playful lace insets at the hems. She tipped her head. *Okay, so casual chic.* She did love her wardrobe. Half of which she'd left at home in her walk-in closet. She searched for the three-strapped sandals, slid them on and buckled.

Noah crawled to the bed, pulled himself up and cruised the rest of the way along the mattress and frame to reach her. He was so close to walking but hadn't as yet dared to take his first step. She picked him up. "Hi, sweetie." He fussed in her arms. "Ready to eat?"

After she put him in his high chair, he fussed more as she prepared his dinner. A timer went off.

"Oh, hold on, Noah. It's time to put in the casserole." He let out an impatient yelp, and she tried to distract him by putting on the large oven mittens, using them as puppets, and making a silly face as her hands talked to each other. It didn't work. She put the dish in the oven, set the timer for forty-five minutes and shortly thereafter started feeding her son.

Not even food helped him settle down, though he ate every bite. Maybe he was teething again?

"One last bite," she said, offering the small spoon filled with soft angel hair pasta cut in half-inch segments with bits of chicken in a creamy marinara sauce. After taking the final bite he let out a grumpy squeal, spitting it far enough to land on her sweater. Then he cried.

Eva didn't waste time cleaning off her top. She jumped right in to lift Noah out of the chair and hold him. "What's wrong?" He cried more. She felt his forehead, but he didn't seem hot. There was too much leftover food in his mouth to search for signs of a new tooth, so she held him close and sang his favorite song, "Shake My Sillies Out." That didn't help, either. So she checked his diaper. Nothing extra in there. "Does your tummy hurt?" Maybe the sauce was too spicy? More crying. She offered him his sippy cup with water, but he pushed it away.

Heading into the living room, she paced with him as he fussed and pumped his legs. It had to be frustrating not being able to communicate what the problem was, so she kept walking and rocking him. "Are you sleepy?" She glanced at her watch; it was almost time for his usual night night.

She'd broken the first rule she'd learned about kids—*they thrive on routine*—and upset his schedule by putting off his dinner. Now she was paying the price. She took Noah to his portable crib area, thinking she needed to get something more permanent for him. She laid him down on the makeshift changing table and put on a dry extra-absorbent nighttime diaper, then covered him in a cotton onesie. Carrying him into the bathroom, she dampened a washcloth to wipe his face and gums, and only then noticed the tiny white tip of a new tooth. The top lateral incisor would make five.

"Oh, that's the trouble." She let him chew the washcloth with his gums, hoping it would offer some relief. A few minutes later she laid him down, thinking he might need to cry himself to sleep. She checked her watch, willing to give him ten minutes to work things out himself.

Heading immediately to the kitchen, she washed her hands and sweater, but there was a stain. No time to change, though. She set the table. The chicken, rice and vegetable casserole smelled delicious in the oven.

"Bread!" She remembered to stick the mini baguette in the oven for the last five minutes of casserole baking, then rushed around putting all the other accoutrements on the table. Lacy insisted she serve two kinds of dressing for the salad, sea salt and fresh pepper to grind and tabasco sauce for the casserole. Just in case Joe liked extra hot. From her personal experience with him, he did!

The oven timer went off and she donned the big

gloves again and put the bread on the trivet to rest. Then she sliced it and wrapped it up in a serving basket to keep it warm. Last, she took the salad bowl out of the refrigerator and placed it on the table, too.

Dinner was ready. Only one problem: Noah still cried. So she rushed to his side and picked him up, hoping to sing one lullaby and send him off to his dreams before Joe arrived.

But the doorbell rang. Too late, he was here. The sudden sound shifted Noah's crying to wails.

Wonderful.

She rushed to the door, wondering if she'd combed her hair one last time or not after sliding the sweater over her head, and trying her best to console Noah, who struggled in her hold. Frazzled, she swung open the door and saw Joe's smile shift to concern.

"Everything okay?" he asked.

She gave him the does-it-look-like-it stare. "He's teething. Sorry. Come in."

Joe stepped through the threshold and followed her to the kitchen. Having been in this situation with a teething baby before, she went about business as usual. Though she was surprised that in his position, he hadn't gone running for the hills when he had the chance. "Would you like something to drink?"

She used one hand to hold Noah and the other to open the refrigerator.

"Let me do that," Joe said, jumping to action.

"Oh, I'm used to working with one hand," she

said, wishing tonight wasn't the night Noah sprang a new tooth.

"Let me get the drinks," he insisted, so she stepped back. "Looks like you could use some wine. Good thing I brought some."

Distracted with Noah, Eva hadn't noticed the bottle until that moment. With Noah not letting up in the fussy department, she liked the idea. "Yes, please."

Joe expertly opened the wine, and even while dealing with a cranky kid, Eva watched the muscles in his forearms as he expertly uncorked the bottle and poured them both some crispy white something or other. His strong hands wrapped around the glass stems, the man-size watch catching her attention as he gave her one. He smelled good, too, wearing some kind of aftershave that bit the air and reminded her of citrus and spices. It blended well with the scent of the Desitin she'd smeared all over Noah's bottom a few moments ago.

Joe's thick hair had been trimmed since she'd last seen him, and fell perfectly into place, a well-placed wave here and there on top, the sides short. Having gone casual, as she had, he wore jeans and a black V-necked T-shirt, revealing a fine gold chain around his neck, the bottom of which was hidden under his shirt. She didn't remember seeing the chain the night they were together. But then, she'd been significantly distracted.

"Let me have him," Joe said, after taking a quick

drink of wine and placing the glass on the counter. "So you can finish whatever you need to do now."

"I'm not sure he'll go to you," she said, but letting him reach for Noah, who, surprisingly went into his arms without a fight.

"Hey, guy. What's up?"

"He's teething."

"So you said." Joe stuck his knuckle in Noah's mouth and let him go to town gumming it. Then he walked him into the living room, where the large front window was open. From the kitchen, as Eva rushed around putting last-minute touches on the table and trying not to forget anything, she glanced into the other room. Joe had stopped in front of the window to show Noah some hummingbirds sampling the white flowers on the huge hibiscus bush. Noah had quieted down some and watched where Joe pointed. "See? Right there."

Eva took her glass of wine and leaned against the kitchen door frame, sipping and enjoying the interaction between Noah and Joe with a smile. Her son let out a huge yawn. They might get to eat before the casserole got cold after all.

"Car," Joe said. "See?"

Noah pointed and pumped his legs at the approaching car lights as it drove by. Then Noah turned his head to watch Joe, and Joe looked back, each taking the other in at close range. "Hi," Joe said in a soft voice. "You look sleepy. Want to lie down?"

Taking Eva's breath away, Joe cupped Noah's head and her son rested on Joe's shoulder, as though he'd been hypnotized and had fallen under some spell. Joe continued to watch him, then after a few moments he glanced up at Eva. "He's out," Joe whispered.

Surprised, Eva headed to them to take her son, but Joe used his head to indicate he'd carry him to bed. She led the way to the alcove tucked in the far end of the hallway, where Joe gently placed the boy on the thin mattress. Eva covered him and then turned to study Joe's gaze. He seemed relaxed and a little in awe of the bundle that was already curled up and out to the world under the thin blanket. His expression tied a tender knot in her chest. Not willing to risk Noah waking, Eva took Joe's hand to lead him away toward the kitchen, soon realizing her mistake in touching him.

Joe hadn't had a woman lead him anywhere for a while. Their time in the limousine didn't count because their fantasy scene had been completely unplanned. Though it had been amazing.

Eva's soft hand in his was a reminder how good human touch was for a person's well-being. For years he'd gotten wrapped up in his law practice and then becoming mayor, letting relationships get put on the back burner. Then he'd wonder why whatever spark he'd originally shared with his dates went out.

It was the simple things that mattered, like fixing

a meal and sharing it, or taking someone's hand after putting a baby to bed. Wait, he'd *never* been in that situation before. Yet holding the boy seemed to come naturally, and studying the baby up close had been nothing short of fascinating. Noah's flawless skin and silky black hair were something in themselves, but his natural interest in everything was what had impressed Joe the most. Babies saw everything as if for the first time. Everything was new for them. With these thoughts flowing he glanced at Eva.

She must have realized it was a mistake to hold his hand—the effect it had on him—so she let it drop. He was sorry.

Without saying a word, he sat at the dinner table and watched as she served the steaming and delicious-smelling casserole to his plate, passed warm bread and then the large wooden bowl of baby greens salad to dish out himself. He'd shared plenty of meals with women, but this one, in the small kitchen of a home laid out identical to his, seemed far more intimate.

"Looks great," he said, meaning it. His mouth watered from the rich mixture of chicken, spices and sauce.

"Thanks." She took a bite. "I'm not going to lie. Lacy put it together for me. I'm more of an order-in kind of person."

He laughed lightly. "That makes two of us. Good thing Lacy's your sister." Then he took another bite of chicken and rice in a creamy yet tangy sauce, truly grateful for Lacy's culinary skills.

"This really is good," Eva agreed, her blue eyes widening with approval.

He'd been around Lacy several times and found her red hair interesting, but with Eva, the color and the texture transfixed him. Her pale complexion, evidence of how little time she spent in the sun, was in stark contrast to his own light brown skin. How else were they different?

"Funny how that works," she said, pulling him out of his thoughts. "Lacy and I are identical physically, but our personalities couldn't be more different."

"I've noticed." Lacy was the bubbly extrovert and Eva far more serious. "Environment accounts for a lot of our character development. It only makes sense that with her growing up around a dad who owned a food truck and cooked for a living, she'd take interest."

The subtle shift in Eva's eyes made him worry he'd somehow put his foot in his mouth.

"He was my dad, too, but I never knew." She pushed food around her plate and stared at it.

"That's got to be hard." His father had influenced Joe's entire life.

"I would've liked to have been given the chance. I would've liked to grow up with my sister in this house and, well, maybe I'd be a good cook, too. Who knows?" She shrugged. "Everything got nipped in the bud and I had zero control over it."

Her frustration was obvious. "I can look into the adoption for you. Find out how it happened. Not that it would change anything, but it may help explain why they, meaning all the adults involved in the arrangement, chose to do what they did."

She hesitated, fork left halfway to her mouth. "You're right, knowing why wouldn't change anything. Lacy and I both went through life feeling part of us was missing. Does everyone feel like that? I can't possibly know, because it's the only thing I know for sure, and she understands."

"No. I don't think everyone feels that way. I think it was definitely related to your being separated at birth."

Things went quiet. Eva ate, but she was obviously dealing with difficult thoughts. There simply was no way to understand what had happened to her without firsthand information.

"Maybe your birth mother is still alive. What information do you have?"

"Me? Nothing. I've tried to get ahold of my mother to make her level with us, but she conveniently dodges me. Maybe if she saw Lacy and me together it would jolt her into coming clean. All she ever told me was I was adopted, and it was a closed adoption. I've honestly never been interested in finding my birth mother...until now."

"Why don't we plan a meeting, the three of us with your mother. Don't give up on her."

"Sounds great, but she seems to be in outer Mongolia or outer space, who knows. She's either not getting my emails or choosing not to answer them. I don't have international service, so I can't call her. You'd think she'd take an interest in her grandson, but maybe my being adopted, and Noah also being adopted is once too far removed for her to care?"

He couldn't let her think so negatively. "She cares. Otherwise why would she adopt you? Keep trying. Set up a time to skype, that's free online, and after you catch up on her travels, we can all get down to business. Find out how much she knows or she's willing to divulge."

Hope brightened Eva's face, and Joe was glad to give it to her. He liked making her smile, having this quiet dinner with her, and even holding Noah. What was that about? Why was he thinking like a family man out of the blue? His reelection campaign had to be first on his list right now, yet he'd offered his services as a lawyer to Eva. Because her mother wasn't the only one who cared. He did, too.

No matter how adamant Eva was about not repeating what they'd done the night they'd met, Joe was convinced she could never be a one-night stand. Not if he could help it.

Pouring more wine, Joe asked for seconds on the dinner, too. Even though Eva hadn't cooked it, he sensed her pride that the meal had gone over well. As for the conversation, he kept things safe after the glimpse of pain Eva, and of course, Lacy, had experienced in life from the secret adoption. Instead, they talked about her nonprofit and his law practice from then on. Though he made it a point to leave out the upcoming election.

After dinner he helped her clean up the table, put the dishes in the washer and store the leftovers, then he got his reward.

"Would you like to watch some TV?"

When was the last time he'd done that? Certainly not since throwing his hat in for reelection. "I'd love to."

"You okay with a BBC crime thriller? I've gotten hooked on one."

"Sure, whatever." Joe was happy to get to spend more time with Eva, no matter what they watched.

They brought the rest of their wine to the living room and shared the couch with a calico cat that appeared out of nowhere.

"That's Daisy, Lacy's cat."

"Hello, Daisy." Joe tried to pet the cat, but she rebuffed him, taking her place on the opposite arm of the couch. He'd seen her around the neighborhood, and a time or two in his backyard, stalking birds. He'd always shooed her off. Did cats remember things like that?

They watched the brilliant London DCI solve a

murder case, all while dealing with extreme personal issues and dishonest coworkers. At some point Joe put his arm along the back of the couch and Eva lightly rested against his chest, obviously wrapped up in the show and forgetting her one rule. He lost all context of the story after that, feeling the warmth of her soft shoulder and inhaling the faint scent of her body lotion. Daisy edged her way between them and curled up, making sure he'd keep his distance. The cat must like their good vibrations, too, because she purred like a motor. He took the moment between the two of them, plus the noisy cat, as a gentle gift, not wanting to test how much more bending of her rule she'd do, yet wanting with everything he had, to find out. He also didn't know when Lacy might come home. Or if at all.

After two episodes, of which he'd retained nothing, they both could no longer conceal their yawns.

"We're like an old married couple," she chastised.

The weird thing was, the thought didn't sound half bad. "That's not so bad, is it?"

"I'm only thirty-one."

"And I've got you beat there, pushing forty. That's what you get hanging out with an old man."

"There's nothing old about you. You're in great shape. I've always thought a man came into his prime in his forties."

"Now you're just making me want to kiss you."

That stopped her. She couldn't deny they'd had

a great time hanging out. They were compatible and attracted to each other—already proved it—and under normal circumstances could be on the threshold of something good. Yet he saw her clear hesitation. Why?

He stood, took her hands and pulled her up, then held her hand as he headed to the door.

"All good things must come to an end," he said, feeling lame. "Dinner was great, so was the company." Feeling even lamer.

She glanced at her feet, bare, the only naked part of her tonight, and he was honest enough to admit he liked when she'd kicked off her shoes while watching TV, secretly wishing she'd take off more. What could he say, he was a guy. "I had a good time, too. I haven't had a relaxing night in like this in forever. So thank you for suggesting it."

"I'd really like to kiss you."

Chapter Eight

Standing in the living room, several feet from the front door, Joe would've been dishonest not to tell Eva how much he wanted to kiss her before he left. So he had.

Her ribs moved with a subtle inhale as she considered her answer, probably worrying what might happen if they did that again. Kissed. For some reason she didn't trust him, or was it men in general? Whatever the reason, he would have to prove himself. Part of that seemed too familiar, as in Victoria Harrington redo, and his never being good enough for her. Not his kisses, no, she'd really liked those, it was just him and his humble upbringing she couldn't get past.

But Eva was a completely different person from fellow rich girl Victoria. Eva was someone doing good work for the community, and someone dealing with a mega surprise—never knowing she was a twin until recently. She was nothing like Victoria.

An idea popped into his head. "How about hands off? A hands-off kiss." He held his up, in evidence. He'd promised to start over, slower this time, and he'd meant it, even if the more time he spent around Eva, he didn't like that idea.

She laughed at his ridiculous suggestion.

"What? I'm serious." He gave a deadpan stare, giving her time for his idea to sink in. "Want to try it? Could be fun." He sensed she did want to, but needed to hear it for himself. "You might like it," he gently taunted. "We could start a whole new thing. Hands-free kissing."

She gave a beguiling glance. "You're crazy, you know that?"

Not backing down, he lifted his brows, waiting for the nod. She thought a second longer.

"Okay," she said. Not the most convincing approval, but he'd take it.

"You have to promise to keep your hands off me, too." That got another laugh from Eva, as if it was the most absurd request, but it helped her relax, so that was good.

"This really is silly." She looked interested, though. Definitely interested.

"But you'll do it?" He secretly held his breath.

She didn't break contact with his gaze, which was an unexpected reward. "Yes."

Ah, the magic word, consent! Victory had never been so sweet. He kept his hands raised, as though following a police command, and stepped toward her, before she could change her mind. She put her hands behind her back but lifted her face to his in readiness. Her eyes studied the ceiling, as she tried not to laugh. He waited until she got that out of her system, and her gaze traveled back to him with a what-are-we-waiting-for challenge, then he let her know how serious he was.

"Our first start-over kiss," he whispered just before he pressed his mouth to hers, immediately reeling at the softness of the lips he'd stared at a good part of the evening. She kissed him tenderly, and he savored the innocent sensation of only having their mouths touch. He angled his head to get closer, yet keeping a wide distance between their bodies. He took his time, exploring the lips he'd once devoured, offering only chaste kisses this time around. A tiny sound emanated from her throat, and he thought he might lose it, but he kept his hands raised, though admittedly closer to clutching her shoulders. What he'd give for a tight hug, to feel her next to him. But her mouth was more than enough for a first step. It had to be, because with Eva, he had something to prove. He'd dream about this sweet kiss the rest of the night. Then she parted her lips and he thought he'd been invited to heaven.

"Mmm…" He couldn't help the sound as he deepened the kiss, hands hovering just above her shoulders.

Unfortunately, his sound effect was enough to make Eva step back. He saw dreamy eyes staring at him, much like how he assumed his looked.

"I don't know if it's because we had prior practice or not," he said, "but that was the best first kiss ever."

Her secret smile, gently twitching at the corners of her mouth, proved she agreed. They stared at each other for several moments, all kinds of sensations sparking over him.

Prove yourself.

"Okay, I better leave. Now." He turned and headed out the door without another word but hoping with all he had that she'd stop him.

On Thursday afternoon, Eva and Noah paid Savannah a visit at her senior living apartment. Noah was visibly impressed with the ceramic dog guarding the apartment door.

"Da!" Noah squealed.

"Yes," Eva encouraged him, and they pet the dog together.

Then he heard the real thing on the other side, barking and growling like a vicious watchdog. He got scared making his pre-crying face. Eva bent down to comfort him before he broke into a full-blown wail. "It's okay. That's just Nipsey."

He seemed to accept her explanation, though not having a clue who Nipsey might be. But, evidently if Momma said it was okay, he believed her.

Savannah opened her door, and at the sight of Noah standing and leaning on the dog, patting the statue's long nose and repeating, "Da! Da!" she clapped her hands and laughed.

"What a doll!" Savannah said, Nipsey yelping and fighting for freedom from her arm.

Once Eva and Noah got settled inside the apartment, after Savannah put the dog in the bedroom and closed the door, she served lemonade and short-bread cookies. While Noah happily crawled around the room, Eva kept watch as she broached the reason for her visit.

"I won't be able to take you to Mayor Aguirre's rally at the high school this weekend. I'm so sorry."

"Don't worry about me, I can find a way there. I'm sure one of the other people here will attend."

Worried that Savannah might get lost, Eva had come to persuade her to sit this one out. "Do you think that's a good idea?"

"I've lived in Little River Valley for forty years. I know the blue line route like the veins on the back of my hands."

What about the dementia? "I could pick you up

and drop you at the school, maybe arrange for someone to meet you there and look after you."

"If you're going to all that effort, why not just
come with me?"

She may as well come clean. "An unfortunate
situation has occurred."

Savannah screwed up her face. "What is that supposed to mean?"

"Someone is making a big deal about Joe and
me on some social media page, and we agreed we
shouldn't be together in public for a while."

"How so? Making a big deal, I mean." Savannah's
face stayed scrunched and questioning.

"By posting our picture with Noah. Insinuating
we are a couple and Noah is Joe's love child. You
know, pure gossip."

Savannah folded her arms, scowling. "Reminds
me of Rona Barrett."

It was Eva's turn to twist her face. "Who's that?"

"A big Hollywood gossip columnist who used
to be on TV. First there was Hedda Hopper, then
Louella Parsons, both before my time. Then Rona
came along."

She'd never heard of any of them, but the one
name, Louella, sent a chill down her spine. What if
Louella Barnstable was behind the website?

"This social media person calls herself Kitty Mittens."

That made Savannah belly laugh and palm the

table, causing the lemonade to vibrate. "Who'd listen to anyone with a name like that? At least in my day the gossips appeared on TV or wrote their columns using their real names."

"Wish it was still the case, but... So, I hope you understand why I can't go onstage with you. Joe would still love to have you there, especially since he's got some great announcements to make concerning senior citizens."

"But it seems so out of your way."

Eva reached for her friend's hand and squeezed. "I feel responsible for you, and I'd be happy to drop you off and then pick you up afterward."

"Thanks, but I'll find my own way home."

"Oh, wait, maybe Joe's campaign manager, Mike, can arrange to get you home?"

"Well, if it meant you didn't have to make two trips on my account, I'm fine with that."

"It's just that the rally happens smack in the middle of Noah's nap."

"Little man needs his sleep, huh, Noah?" Savannah made big eyes and grinned at Noah, who'd managed to crawl over and push the bedroom door open and free the dog. He happily tried to catch Nipsey's tail as he ran around yipping like a circus dog.

After they finished their lemonade and ate the cookies while catching up with each other—Eva leaving out all the good parts that involved Joe—they made plans for Eva to pick up and drop Savannah off at the high school on Saturday. Eva promised to have Mike call and arrange for Savannah to get home. And somehow, Noah and Nipsey had become best playmates, causing tears when it was time to leave.

An hour before the rally at Newton High School on Saturday, Eva, and the car packed with Noah in his car seat in the back and Savannah riding shotgun, pulled to the curb at the arranged drop-off site by the far end of the football field. It was a small school, the only public high school in a town that also housed an exclusive private preparatory school whose annual tuition competed with many top universities. Joe had chosen the everyman's school for the rally. Exactly as Eva would expect.

She had learned since living with Lacy that there was a small but extremely wealthy population in Little River Valley. The private school was known nationwide, and many of the local kids would be at Joe's rally today as a kind of civics assignment if for nothing else. The standard football field outsized the small public high school grounds, whose entire ninth–twelfth grade population numbered around eight hundred. The bleachers could hold at least that, and Eva hoped today they'd be filled for Joe's sake.

Savannah had chattered coherently the entire drive over, about everything from what she'd had for breakfast to how she'd chosen what she wore, which proved she was alert and oriented.

"Savannah, I don't want an argument about me picking you up. Mike will be busy with a million things after the rally, and I'm fine with coming back for you."

"But I thought…"

"I'm living with Lacy now, not all the way up in Santa Barbara. This really isn't a problem."

"So you'll meet me here then?"

She shouldn't have a problem finding her way back to this prearranged spot. Still, Eva felt the need to reinforce the meeting place.

"All you have to do is look for this huge oak tree right here on the corner," Eva said, before letting Savannah out of the car. "Do you want to write down the street names, Brookes and Donner, to help remind you?"

"Brookes and Donner, I know these streets well. That tree will help. I'll be fine."

"Look behind you. See the football field? It's a straight shot."

"Won't be a problem."

"Do you have your sun hat with you? And did you put on sunscreen? Speaking of that, try to find a place in the shade on that stage."

"Yes, Mother," Savannah mocked, but seemed to appreciate Eva caring.

"You remember what Mike looks like, yes?"

"Short, wide guy. Big toothy smile."

That about nailed it. Eva opened her door and got

out to help Savannah to the curb. Driving a low car made it extra hard for people of a certain age to exit. She took both her friend's hands and gave a firm tug to get her started. "There we go."

Savannah grunted on the last part. "Well." She stood tall and gave an assertive nod. "We made it." Eva figured that after a certain age, the little things became achievements.

Strapped in his car seat, Noah kicked his legs and pumped his arms, expecting his turn to get out.

"Sorry, sweetie, this is just a drop-off."

He fussed more.

"Maybe he'd like a little walk around before the drive home," Savannah said.

"It might help him nap better, too," Eva agreed. She bent over the back seat to unlatch her son when footsteps approached from behind.

"Savannah!" It was Joe. Though she'd explained to him about the drop-off, this was not part of the plan.

She hadn't seen him since their amazing no-hands kiss Wednesday. His life and her job had kept them both too busy. Though he had called Thursday around noon to thank her for dinner and the great evening. They'd avoided mentioning their stellar kiss. So far he'd been a perfect and courteous date, and she waited for some missing link to show up. Eva turned quickly and bumped her head on the car's doorframe. "Ouch!" She rubbed her scalp.

"You okay?" Joe asked, concern obvious.

"Fine, fine. Just stings." *Like my pride.* She'd only expected to see Mike today, who was supposed to walk Savannah to the football field, so she'd worn some old workout clothes and hadn't bothered with makeup.

When Eva lifted Noah and hoisted him on her hip, she found Savannah grinning like a schoolgirl at Joe, and Joe, well, looking sinfully sweet as always. Signature working guy's jeans and buttoned shirt, this one's tint making his brown eyes look almost green. Not to mention the boots. Why did they always do something to her? She kept her sigh to herself.

"Where's Mike?"

"I wanted to escort Savannah myself." He winked, giving Eva the impression he'd wanted to see her, too.

Why hadn't she thought about that when getting dressed? "That's awfully nice of you." What wasn't?

"Isn't he the most thoughtful man?" Savannah chimed in, clearly reading her mind.

"Absolutely." Still wishing she'd made a different fashion choice.

"Hey, Noah. How are you, buddy?" Noah grinned and kicked in delight at Joe's greeting and didn't resist a bit when Joe reached for him. "Want to take a walk?" He let Noah down on the lawn and held his hands as he walked on his tiptoes as though the grass blades bothered him.

"Does it tickle?" Eva giggled at the sight. Noah

didn't seem to care if she laughed at him or not, because he was hanging out with his new best friend, the guy who put him to bed the other night.

"How's that tooth doing?"

He remembered. Considerate as always. "It's mostly through the gum. Thank goodness."

Joe picked him up and swung him around, while Noah squealed with joy. After giving sufficient attention to her tot, Joe handed him back and grew serious.

"I wanted to be the one to show you this," he said, digging out his cell phone from his back pocket and scrolling through some pages before handing her a picture. "I have no idea how they got it, but it's beginning to feel like stalking."

There was Joe, holding Noah, standing in the window at Lacy's. A chill ran through her as she remembered him pointing out a car for her son. The caption said, "Love child in Mayor Daddy's arms." "This is insane! They can't do that, spread sheer lies, can they? You're the lawyer."

"They aren't allowed to trespass or use telephoto lenses, but they never got out of the car and, as you can tell by the grainy pixels, they used a cell phone zoom in and cropped it closer afterward."

"That's crummy, and completely unfair." Eva had a list of choice words she'd like to blurt to describe the low-life paparazzi's invasion of their privacy, but since having Noah, she'd learned to eat the most descriptive ones.

"I suppose I could pursue whoever this is with libel for stating Noah is my child. If I knew who it was."

"Isn't there a way to find out who Kitty Mittens's Facebook page belongs to?"

"There probably is, but honestly, I don't have time for that now. And some third party could be feeding her the photos. So here's how I want to deal with this." He turned and motioned toward Savannah. "Will you take our picture, please?"

Eva froze. "But I look like hell—" she glanced at Noah "—I mean heck!"

"You always look beautiful, no matter what. Come on, step in here, while I hold Noah." He handed Savannah his phone and showed her how to take the picture. She looked uncertain but stepped back and held the phone like an old-fashioned camera up to her eye.

"Look at the screen, darlin', not through the lens. Turn it around." So patient. "There, see us?"

"Oh!" Savannah, looking a little flustered by her error, took a wide stance as though technique was key when a person wasn't quite sure of what they were doing. "Smile pretty!"

Though upset by what was obviously turning into a smear campaign against Joe, Eva was still able to smile from her heart because of two things: he'd told her in a roundabout way she was beautiful, and he'd called Savannah darlin' without the g. Who could hold a grudge against a great guy like that for forcing her to take a picture without makeup?

"What are you going to do with that?" Eva asked the instant it was taken.

Joe took back his phone and showed Eva the final product for her approval. "See? Beautiful," he said with a blunt stare. She'd also noticed how gorgeous he looked in the photo. As in hunk-handsome. "I'm going to post it at my reelection website with the caption 'Newest supporters.'" He lifted his brows while waiting for her approval. "You are going to vote for me, right?"

She laughed. "I'm not even a resident here, but my double is definitely voting for you."

He gave Noah a deadpan stare. "I guess that means you aren't voting for me, either." Noah clamped his hands onto Joe's face and squeezed his cheeks in answer. "Well, I can't win everyone over, can I?" He gazed at Eva who worried he could read her mind. *You're doing a great job of winning me over.* "After today's announcement, I should be getting lots more senior citizens' support, though."

"The locals are supporting the senior discounts for breakfast?"

"And some, even lunch, and I have a list of the businesses who have signed on to thank today."

Savannah clapped her hands. "Makes me want to start having breakfast out again."

"I can arrange that first thing Monday morning, and have the *Voice* there to record it, too." Mike had showed up as promised. He bent his arm for Savannah to latch on to. "Shall we get going? Joe, kiss your girl and say goodbye. The rally starts in twenty minutes."

Eva's cheeks heated with the point-blank phrase. His girl? Joe looked mildly sheepish, too, with his best friend being insensitive to their walk-it-back romance. It made her wonder and worry how much Joe had shared with Mike. But there wasn't time for a discussion now, the man had a rally to run.

"So I'll be right here to pick Savannah up at three. Mike, can you make sure she gets here?"

"Absolutely."

"See you, then." Grateful for the team effort, Eva smiled at Savannah, who was happily on her way with Mike toward the makeshift stage at the far end of the football field. She might be in early dementia, but her legs were in great shape and she had no problem keeping up with Mike's short-legged pace.

Savannah turned and winked at Eva. "See you later." She seemed to be someone walking on air, feeling important, or was it because Joe had called her darlin'? Whatever, the effect it had on the woman made Eva smile.

Joe handed Noah back to Eva. "Though I'd really like to kiss you again, I won't dare in public."

She thought of the huge hibiscus bush that covered half of Lacy's front porch and wondered if they could take a rain check on that kiss behind it, later. It must've made her expression change.

"What," Joe said, obviously reading her mischievous eyes.

"If you want to reschedule—" she scratched a sudden itch on her scalp "—I know a place where no paparazzi could angle a shot."

His brows arched. "I'd like to hear all about that secret place. Can I call later?"

She nodded. Looking like he definitely wanted to kiss her on the spot, he took a step back, then pivoted around, ready to head for the rally.

"Knock 'em dead!" she said.

"You know it!" Off he swaggered in those boots like a man full of pride and great ideas. She allowed herself to stand there and watch him, too, until Noah decided he'd had enough.

Three hours later, Noah had taken a great nap and Eva had used her time wisely on Dreams Come True business, putting the finishing touches on her next granted wish. As planned, she drove up to the corner of Brookes and Donner, parked by the huge oak tree, and waited for Savannah to show up.

She waited. And waited. And just when she was ready to call Mike, her cell chirped.

"It's Mike. I've lost track of Savannah. Is she there with you?"

Chapter Nine

The hour following Joe's successful rally was spent
searching for Savannah. He'd been pumped by the
size of the crowd and the cheers for his latest news
about discounted breakfasts throughout Little River
Valley. Several small businesses had signed on,
gladly, not wanting to have to compete with outside
fast food, which could threaten their business if the
Change the Charter supporters had their way. Discounts were proven ways to drive more people to
restaurants, and a happy customer could become a
regular. Which was the main goal. Win-win.

He'd figured Savannah had set off with Mike for
her rendezvous with Eva as planned, until Mike appeared shamefaced at his side.

"One minute she was here, the next she wasn't," Mike said, looking flummoxed. "I saw her in a heated conversation with some other seniors right over there." He pointed to the area to the west of the stage. "I figured she'd wait there for me, like we'd planned, so I took a moment to give a statement to the reporter from the *Voice*. Next thing I know, all the old folks are gone, and Savannah wasn't there."

"She was in a *heated* conversation?" Joe couldn't imagine Savannah arguing with anyone.

"Looked like it. Some of them had signs."

"Change the Charter signs?"

"Yeah, those guys."

Thinking fast, Joe added up the situation. "Doesn't Louella bus them in? Where's the bus?"

"It *was* over there," Mike said, pointing to the back of the stage in the school parking lot.

Several buses from various groups had parked there earlier, and now only two were left. Joe's sinking feeling worsened as he and Mike marched toward them. Eva had trusted him to keep track of Savannah. Though the woman seemed alert and with it, he needed to remember she was in early dementia, which meant she could get easily confused. After a quick check, they were sure neither of the remaining buses had Savannah on board.

"Louella's bus isn't here. Maybe she went with them. Do you have any idea where they come from?"

"The senior center?" Mike shrugged.

"Are you sure or guessing?"

"Guessing, but doesn't it make sense?"

"Yeah, but we can't go on a wild-goose chase when Savannah might be wandering around right under our noses, lost and confused."

"I'll check it out," Mike said. "You stay here. Oh, and I'll call Eva to let her know the plan."

Joe's stomach double-knotted; the last thing he wanted to do was cause Eva stress. He'd selfishly wanted Savannah onstage as his senior representative because Mike had convinced him she played well with the public, and now she was gone.

He cupped his hands beside his mouth. "Savannah!" he yelled, after Mike darted off for his car to check out the senior center. "Savannah!"

With concern deepening, he looked around, grabbed a nearby high school girl who'd volunteered to pass out leaflets. "Can you check all the ladies' rooms for Savannah, the senior woman who was on the stage with me?"

With only a nod, off the teenager trekked toward the gym and the restrooms, obviously happy to help.

Joe hiked back and stood at the front of the stage on the football field and systematically scanned the surroundings, making a complete circle. There was no sign of Savannah, and the crowd had thinned enough to see she wasn't anywhere in the vicinity. It would be hard to miss her straw hat and red blouse.

He extracted his cell phone from his back jeans pocket and called Eva.

"Joe? Have you found her?" Panic punctuated her words.

"Sorry. Not yet. But Mike's on his way to the senior center. And I have a girl checking all the bathroom stalls."

"I should never have left her on her own." Remorse painted the words. "Savannah lives in the independent section of the assisted-living apartments, but they still keep close watch on their coming and going. She signed out earlier when I picked her up, so on the long shot she's already signed back in at the apartments, I'll check. I feel a little sick for trusting her more than I should have."

"It's not your fault. It's mine. Stay where you are for a while longer, maybe she's making her way to you." He hoped for a miracle. If anything happened to Savannah, he'd be completely responsible, and Eva would never forgive him. The idea, on both counts, made him queasy.

Not giving up, he continued to check out every part of the stage and the football bleachers.

The volunteer came back. "She isn't in the bathrooms, and I checked inside and out. I even had a guy check the men's rooms."

"Okay, thanks." Joe's cell rang. It was Mike. "I want good news."

"You got it. She was on the bus with the other seniors and is here at the center."

"Thank God!"

"She said they told her to get on the bus and she thought that was what she was supposed to do."

The old judging a book by the cover saying never rang truer. Savannah looked sharp, like she had things together, and most of the time she did, but today, left on her own in a large crowd for a few minutes, she'd gotten confused. "I'll call Eva. You bringing her back?"

"On our way now."

Joe thanked the staff for all the work they'd done and jogged off across the football field to find Eva. She was leaning against the passenger-side car door watching Noah crawl around in the grass, her arms folded, her forehead creased, when he approached. She anxiously watched him, and his first impulse was to beg her to forgive him for freaking her out.

"Mike found her at the senior center." He wasted no time, called out the information twenty feet out.

She clapped her hands to her mouth, obviously relieved, but also looking confused. He rushed the final steps to her. Out of breath, he took her in his arms, hugged and released her, though wanting nothing more than to keep her near. But who knew who was around waiting for the next photo op? "Someone told her to get on the bus, so she did."

"Oh my God. She totally forgot our plans."

"Apparently." Unable to resist, his arm went around her shoulders and tugged her to his side.

"It's my fault," Eva said, looking up at him as though waiting for him to cast blame. "Short term memory goes first. I should know that."

"No. It's mine." He took full responsibility.

"It's my fault!" Mike called out as he popped out of his car after parking in front of Eva's.

Savannah emerged from the passenger side. "No, it was my fault. One minute I was arguing with the Change the Charter crowd, and the next I'm being hustled off to a bus. They told me to get on and I did. No questions asked."

Eva ran to Savannah and they hugged. "I totally forgot I was supposed to meet you here," Savannah continued. "I'm *so* sorry."

"It's okay, Savannah," Eva said, patting her arm and then holding her hands. "We found you and you're okay. That's all that's important."

Tears brimmed in Savannah's eyes and Eva's went all watery. And Joe never wanted to make her cry again.

"Now let's drive you home," Eva said, putting her arm around the woman's waist and edging her toward the car.

"I'm coming, too," Joe insisted.

Later, after Savannah was safely delivered home, where Nipsey eagerly waited for a pee break, Eva drove to Lacy's. Joe hopped out, then got Noah out of the back before Eva had a chance. They'd only talked about the rally on the drive home, avoiding the subject hanging heaviest on his heart.

"I feel like I betrayed your trust," he said, handing Noah to her.

"That's a little dramatic," she said flippantly. "Didn't know you were a drama queen."

Not the reaction he'd expected. "I promised she'd be looked after, and she got lost."

"And I believed she'd remember where the oak tree was at Brookes and Donner. We both messed up. So don't try to take all the blame." She hugged Noah close and kissed him, as though he'd been the one who'd gone missing.

"It'll never happen again," he said.

"Agreed." She started for Lacy's front porch.

He stayed put. Not wanting to assume he could follow her inside. "You gonna be around tomorrow?" Though hopeful, he suspected she might not want to see him.

"Should be. Lacy, Noah and I have some plans" was all she said as she pulled the screen open and unlocked the door with Noah balanced on her hip. She glanced over her shoulder as she entered, checking to see where Joe was.

He pointed to his house, assuming she'd rather be alone right about then, then lifted a hand to say goodbye, a strong sense of dereliction of duty following him home.

* * *

Sunday afternoon, Joe had run a couple of errands, showered, shaved and slapped on extra aftershave, then trudged two doors down to find Eva. He rapped on the door. Lacy answered. He immediately knew it was her, though it still startled him how identical they were. Thank goodness they wore their hair differently. "Eva here?" He kept his hands behind his back.

"Sure, come in."

"Nope, I'll wait here, thanks."

Lacy glanced toward his side, trying hard to see around him, a suspicious smile brightening her face. "Let me get her."

Checking out the neighborhood, watching for any stray cars in the vicinity, Joe also eyed the huge hibiscus bush that concealed half of the front porch. *Perfect.*

A couple moments later, Eva came to the screen, without Noah, thankfully. Joe wanted her all to himself for the next few minutes. "Hi," she said, opening the screen for him to enter.

He used his head to gesture for her to step out and then moved, walking backward, toward the bush.

She followed him into the bushy cave, checking him out head to boots. "You smell good."

"Thank you." He went halfway behind the hibiscus, a place no one could grab a picture, and pulled out the huge bouquet. "I think these are what smell good." He'd had the florist throw in every scent-intensive flower she had. "I am so sorry for yesterday."

Obviously touched by his gesture, she took the flowers, smelled them, then eagerly stepped into his open arms. He drew her near, getting caught up in the feel of her, how perfectly she fit with him, her warmth. After nuzzling her hair, he planted a well-placed kiss on her mouth, sensing her relax, then kiss him back. His fingers dug into her hair as he angled his head and parted her lips, discovering the taste he couldn't get out of his head since the night he'd met her. From there, they went for it, kissing the heck out of each other, like starving lovers, complete with throat noises and moans bouncing off the bush and front porch wall, the sounds only egging them on.

It was a good thing they were outside and standing up, otherwise they might've wound up like they had that night in the limousine.

What was it about Evangelina that drove him mad?

A few minutes later, after they'd come to their senses—mainly because Eva had dropped the bouquet and Joe nearly tripped on it when he'd leaned back on the porch rail to pull Eva closer—Joe stopped the kiss. There was nowhere to go from here except tearing each other's clothes off and jumping straight into bed, and that wasn't going to happen, not with Lacy and Noah inside.

"You want to come to my house?"

"I'd really like to, but we have birthdays to celebrate."

That pulled him out of his sex-starved haze. "It's
your birthday?"

"No. Noah's. He's one. And on Sunday after-
noons, Lacy and I make up for all the birthdays we've
missed." Her forearms rested on his shoulders, his
hands on her waist.

"You and Lacy?" Why did the fact that sisters
who never got to share birthdays were making up for
it now chink away at his heart?

"Lacy bakes a cake, we sing to ourselves and tell
each other what we remember about those years.
Today we're celebrating ages six through ten, and
I'm pretty sure the cake will have a unicorn on it
since we discovered we both loved them at that age."

He couldn't stop the smile. "I'm really glad you
two found each other."

She nodded. He was glad he and Eva had found
each other, too. Thanks to Savannah. Which was
why he'd come to apologize today. Having come full
circle, he let her go and stood.

"What about Noah?"

"He gets his own and his cupcake has Thomas
the Tank Engine on it."

"No big first birthday party?"

"We just came from Zack and Emma's. Celebrated
there."

Feeling left out without a legitimate reason, he

smiled anyway. "Wish I'd known. I'd like to get him a present."

"That's sweet of you, and Noah will be thrilled whenever. You know, no sense of time at one. Oh," she said, "I was going to call and tell you, I've tracked down my mom and we have a Skype date tonight. Any chance you can be here for legal input?"

"Absolutely. What time?"

"Seven."

"At the risk of finding you both full of cake, can I bring some takeout to share at six?"

"I'd love that." She hugged him, kissed him lightly, then bent to pick up the trampled-on bouquet. "And thank you for these," she said before heading back inside. "I'll save you a piece of cake. Oh, and thanks for understanding about the birthday make-ups, and needing to do that together."

Joe absolutely did understand, even though he couldn't begin to fathom what it must be like finding a twin after all the lost years. He sat on the railing for a few more moments, letting the obvious reaction from her kisses wear off before he went home.

"Okay, where'd we leave off," Eva said, joining her sister in the kitchen as she iced the second cake of the day.

"Oh no. You don't get off that easily," Lacy said, stopping mid icing spread. "What just happened out there on the porch?"

Eva pulled inward for a moment. Did Lacy have a right to know every little thing that went on in her life because they were living together? Not that kissing the face off Joe just then would ever qualify as a "little thing." Or did Lacy feel she had the right to know because they were sisters? This was all new territory, and sometimes Eva tensed under the constant scrutiny. Maybe it was time to let Lacy know. "I'm going to be honest. I've lived my whole life as an only child, and I'm not used to sharing every little aspect of my life."

"I'm being too nosy, you mean? Again?" Lacy gave a self-deprecating laugh. "It's my nature. Dad was that way, too. Always had to know everything. Sorry if I'm overstepping my bounds."

Immediately Eva regretted her words, since Lacy had been trying so hard to make up for lost time. "Please don't get offended. I'm the one with issues, not you."

Lacy stopped decorating the cake and turned to give Eva her full attention. "We both have issues because of what they did to us. I want so badly to be a real sister to you, the kind I used to dream about, but I don't really know how to, never had the practice, and I don't want to push you away because of it."

Part of Eva's icy defense melted with the statement. "I understand." Eva stepped closer to Lacy and put a hand on her shoulder. "I promise to work harder at sharing more with you."

"Thanks for understanding." Lacy peered over her shoulder with an impish gaze. "You could start right now, by telling me if Joe's as great a kisser as I think he is?"

Eva blurted a laugh, unlike her usual reserve, then lightly cuffed her sister on the arm. "Good try. But I'd like to hold on to that secret just a little longer."

"You are such a stickler."

"And you're a busybody."

Bickering had never been more fun.

If it hadn't been for Eva's persistence, Bridget DeLongpre may never have been convinced to chat live online. Being vain, she'd left her cruise ship stateroom dim, making it hard to see her features. Her white hair was pulled back in a hairband, paging under a few inches below her ears. Though she smiled, it was clear to Eva she was tense.

"It's shocking seeing you two together," she said after the introductions.

"You can't imagine," Eva added. She glanced at Lacy. "She's the best and biggest surprise of my life."

"I'm thrilled you discovered each other."

"Really?" Eva questioned her sincerity. How could she be thrilled when she'd spent all of Eva's life hiding the truth from her?

"Eva, it was a closed adoption at the gestational surrogate's request." She'd obviously picked up on

Eva's doubtful sentiment. "I gave the surrogate my word."

This was new information, information that sent ice down her spine. "A surrogate? Our mother was paid to get pregnant?"

For some crazy reason, all these years Eva had assumed her mother had found a baby offered for adoption by someone who never meant to get pregnant.

"To help a family have a child they'd longed for, and inadvertently giving me the chance to be a parent," Bridget corrected.

Joe lightly clinched Eva's tensed shoulder, reassuring her he was nearby, ready and willing to help her understand their complete story. Lacy, who sat beside Eva in front of the computer monitor, reached for and squeezed her hand. She'd never felt more protected in her life, yet still vulnerable.

At last they were getting to the truth, which was already hard to hear.

After the brief silence, Bridget sighed. "Yes. John and Elaine had tried for I think around fifteen years to have a baby, and finally decided to seek a surrogate, since Elaine was starting early menopause. The surrogate was artificially inseminated by your father, Lacy."

"You met my parents?" Lacy squeezed Eva's hand tighter as she asked.

"We met when the surrogate brought me in."

Eva's chest went hot with adrenaline, her breath quickening; she was unready but willing to hear the truth for the first time. "Mom, could you please tell us the story from the start?"

Bridget took a long drink of something, then nodded. "So John and Elaine were desperate to have a baby around the same time I wanted to adopt. Since adoption agencies preferred married couples to single women, I looked into the option of surrogacy. My name was put on some list, and out of the blue I got a call from a surrogate who was already pregnant. I had planned to choose a sperm donor from a bank where I could pick the traits that I wanted, both physical and mental. So at first, I hesitated. Sorry if that's disappointing to you, Eva, but I wanted a designer baby. Actually, that probably doesn't surprise you."

Eva held her honest reaction in check. If anyone would try for a designer baby, it would be Bridget. Perhaps that was the beginning of her mother's disappointment in having adopted Eva, she wasn't designer enough?

"No, Mom, it makes sense." Perfect sense. There was no animosity in her comment, just a recognition of the mother she'd grown up with, the mother who'd adopted her and given her everything in life, the mother she loved regardless of her unintentional superficiality on occasion.

Lacy's clutch of Eva's hand strangled the blood

from her fingers, but she wouldn't let go, needing the support of her twin.

"John and Elaine's surrogate found out she was pregnant with twin girls, and Lacy, your parents couldn't afford to pay twice as much as they'd planned, which is what she'd asked. So I met with her, and being assured she carried twins, decided I could get what I wanted, a girl, and help this other couple, not to mention the surrogate double her fee. I was nearing forty and didn't want to wait much longer to adopt. So I made my offer, which matched your parents, and we had a deal. A deal where we all agreed to a closed adoption.

"And I am under contractual and legal agreement to never divulge who your mother was. She requested it and we all agreed. I knew very little about her beyond her health status anyway. There was one interesting thing as it turned out, but one I think I can share. She did have one request. I think it was her way of leaving a small legacy. She insisted we both give you the same middle name."

"We wondered how that had happened. So she was married?" Eva needed as much information as she could get. Eva and Lacy had discovered early on they both had the same middle name, Taylor; now they knew why. It was one more thing to piece together. The gestational surrogate adoption using artificial insemination from John Winters, Lacy's dad, also explained why Elaine was the only one who needed to adopt Lacy. Having twins must have been a shock to everyone, until Bridget came on board. Still, it hurt to know Eva had never met her father.

"She wasn't married at that time. She confided in me that she planned to use the money to get a new start somewhere. I got the impression she planned to move out of state after the delivery. I think it's okay to tell you that."

Eva glanced at Lacy, who had tears in her eyes and swallowed down her emotion. "You don't know where she might have moved?"

Bridget shook her head. "Even if I did, I wouldn't be able to tell you. I've probably said too much already as it is. That's why I've never wanted to talk about it with you."

Eva looked over her shoulder at Joe, who stood behind her, his hand still warm on her shoulder. "So we have no legal recourse to find our mother if she's still alive."

"How old was she?" Lacy asked, tears streaking down her cheeks.

"She was in her early twenties. I'm not exactly sure, but she was in good health, that was legally established early on, and she seemed very nice. She was clearly young and innocent. I did worry that she didn't have a college degree."

Good old superficial Mom.

"So she'd only be in her fifties now. What color hair did she have?" Lacy asked.

"It was blondish. You two clearly got your red hair from John, your father."

It didn't feel freeing to learn this new information, not nearly as much as Eva had hoped. The more questions that were answered the more questions were raised. "Didn't anyone suggest it wasn't a good idea to split us up?" Eva could no longer avoid the question heaviest on her heart.

"If we'd gone with a typical agency adoption, I'm sure they wouldn't allow it, but your birth mother had two babies inside her, and John and Elaine realistically knew they couldn't afford two children. I honestly felt like I was doing everyone, including you, Eva, a favor. We found a lawyer willing to draw up the legal agreement. Though I do recall the nurse at the hospital asking me if I was sure I wanted to separate the two of you. I knew I couldn't handle two babies, and John and Elaine had their hearts set on a baby."

This was no time to argue. It had taken weeks to get Bridget to talk about the adoptions, and now, with her last statement, she was on the verge of tears.

"I will say this," Bridget continued. "Your birth mother went through so much carrying twins. She was so huge by the end that you'd think it was quintuplets. I never saw someone that big. And both of you were healthy because she took great care of herself and wanted to give you both the best from the very beginning. She did worry about splitting up the babies, we all did, and I think that's why she wanted you to have the same middle name. Like it was some secret symbolic bonding between you and her. Out of appreciation for her sacrifice to bear these babies for us, we agreed to her request."

"Were you present at the birth?"

"No. That was her second request. We both waited in different rooms. It was crazy how nervous I was, and labor seemed to take forever. Poor thing."

"You can't give us her first name?" Lacy persisted.

Bridget shook her head. "No. I'm sorry, Lacy." She went quiet for a moment. "I just can't believe how identical you two are. My goodness, it takes my breath away." Her chin quivered as she put her fist to her lips.

"You can imagine how we felt seeing each other for the first time," Eva said. "I thought I was going to faint."

"How did you decide who got which baby?" Lacy apparently was filled with questions, seizing the moment, and Eva, being stunned by the story, was glad Lacy stayed on track.

"I honestly think it came down to the delivery nurse. I don't know how she decided. But obviously healthy beautiful girls were born with copper-red hair and pale blue eyes just like John. So John and Elaine were in one room, and I was in another."

Lacy looked eagerly at Eva and back to the computer monitor. "We already figured out we were born ten minutes apart. I was first, so my parents must have gotten me since they started the whole thing going."

"That makes sense, though I wasn't told your time of birth," Bridget said, clearing her throat, trying to get a grip. "Evangelina Taylor DeLongpre, you were brought to me at 9:28 p.m. and I couldn't believe the precious gift Desirae gave me."

"Desirae? Was that her name or the nurse's?" Eva jumped on the slip.

Bridget looked visibly shaken, which made Eva think she'd accidentally divulged their mother's name. Desirae. Fortunately, it wasn't a common name and would give them something to work with. "The nurse," Bridget quickly clarified, causing a burst of disappointment for Eva. She would go to her grave never knowing who her birth mother was.

One more thing hit her. "But wait, Mom, so you're saying, after the birth, you never saw John and Elaine again?"

"That's right. The deal was done. We were to have zero contact. And we only knew first names. Though you were born in a small hospital in Santa Paula, I had no clue where they lived, and they didn't know I was taking you to Los Angeles."

Santa Paula! Another unintentional slipup, but Eva didn't want to point that out. Her mother might get upset and never talk about it again.

"Where were you raised, Lacy?" Bridget must not have realized her second mistake. Thank goodness.

"Little River Valley."

"Oh, not far from there. Interesting."

"And how did you two finally meet?" It was Bridget's attempt to get out of the hot seat.

Lacy was happy to tell the story of how they'd found each other, while Eva watched her mother's amazed expression.

"People kept telling me I had a doppelgänger, then Zack got a request for a bathroom remodel in Santa Barbara, and his guy insisted I had a double. It really made me wonder what was going on. Then one day I was serving lunch at the construction site and out steps Eva. It was surreal."

The story really did seem impossible, yet they'd been brought together by chance or fate or whatever. All it took was one person knowing one of them and haphazardly seeing the other, which was set off by Eva moving from Los Angeles to Santa Barbara. Who'd have thought the day she'd decided to make that move—when the adoption of Noah had come through—how momentous her decision would be. That it would set off a domino effect that would eventually bring her and her twin together. When her only goal had been to raise Noah in a smaller city, she'd opened the door and taken the first step toward finding her sister. "Obviously my decision to move to Santa Barbara was the best one of my life, after deciding to adopt Noah, of course."

"It certainly seems to be," Bridget said, still looking mildly stunned by the surprising turnaround in the supposedly closed adoption. "I guess some things are meant to be."

Eva glanced at Lacy; they both believed with all their hearts that they were meant to find each other.

"Mom, thank you so much for all of this information. It has helped us understand so much. We really appreciate it."

"Please don't try to find your birth mother," Bridget said, sounding suddenly desperate. "She made it clear she wanted a fresh start."

"I think it would be impossible anyway," Eva said, attempting to reassure her mother, while feeling Joe's fingers tighten on her shoulder. "I'm sure you need to go have dinner or breakfast or whatever time it is there in New Zealand."

"Lunch. I've missed the sit-down, but the buffet is always open." Bridget's forced Realtor smile popped up. "It was good to meet you, Lacy. I look forward to meeting you in person one day."

"Same here," Lacy said.

"I love you, Mom," Eva said, overcome with emotion and, after the extended explanation of their birth circumstances, gratitude.

"You know I love you," Bridget said, the stiff

upper lip gone and her eyes tearing up. "Only ever wanted the best for you."

There probably hadn't been studies available back then showing the psychological damage separating twins or triplets or multiples could have. Lacy and Eva had paid a subtle but lifelong price until they'd found each other. Always feeling incomplete, wondering why they'd both experienced deep loneliness and longing. Lacy pretending to have an invisible sister, Eva always wishing for a sister. It explained so much to them.

"Don't be so hard to track down next time," Eva couldn't help throwing in, reminding her mother of the frustration she'd caused. Though this was nothing compared to their birth, where everyone involved was guilty.

Bridget gave a natural smile, looking relieved they'd finally had this conversation after all these years. "I won't."

The moment the monitor went dark and the connection died, Eva and Lacy reached for each other and held tight, crying. "Money. It was money that kept us apart. Your parents not having enough, our birth mother needing it, and my mother happy to buy a baby."

"And timing," Lacy said, sloppy with tears and a runny nose. "If your mother hadn't been ready to adopt, who knows what would've happened to us.

I would think, that with their backs to the wall, my mom and our dad might've changed their minds."

"We'll never know. At least we've got each other now."

They went back to hugging and crying and rocking each other for comfort. And Eva chided herself for getting annoyed by Lacy's sometimes needy ways. It only made sense she'd hold tight to Eva after missing her for the last thirty years. Secretly Eva thought of one tiny nagging feeling she continued to have. There was *still* something missing inside. She rationalized it was probably because she'd gotten used to the feeling all her life, and like any habit, it was too hard to break now. She'd found her twin; why should she still feel there was something else not quite right. She didn't have the nerve to bring it up with Lacy for fear of hurting her. But what if Lacy felt the same? Why wouldn't it be a good idea to mention it in that case. Undecided what to do, Eva would continue to hold off.

After they'd completed their total meltdown and slow recovery, wiping their tears and blowing their noses, Joe spoke. "We've actually got a wealth of information with the nurse's name, or, in case your mom was covering her tracks, your mother's name, plus your middle name, which could be a maiden name, since your mom insisted the surrogate wasn't married. *And* the records from that small hospital in Santa Paula will give us something, especially since we already have a birth date and the fact that you were twins. We should be able to identify your birth mother fairly easily. Tracking her down might not be much harder."

Eva looked at Lacy, who continued to wipe her eyes, and silently they communicated the same thought, Eva was sure of it. "I think, out of respect for our birth mother, who obviously sacrificed a lot carrying us for nine months and did her best by us, we should accept her wishes not to seek her out."

Lacy hugged Eva and they cried more, in total agreement.

"I'm just glad we found each other," Lacy finally said.

"Me, too."

After another long, fortifying hug Lacy pulled out and looked a little hesitant. "Would you mind if I went to see Zack?"

"Of course not." Eva understood how important Lacy's fiancé was to her, how much she loved him. Especially since Lacy had never expected to find another person to love after losing her first fiancé to the war in the Middle East. Now she had Zack and she needed him. The last thing Eva wanted to do was interfere with the relationship between Lacy and her future husband.

Lacy glanced at Joe. It occurred to Eva that if he wasn't here, Lacy may have not left her alone. Not after the mind-blowing conversation with the one remaining person involved in their surrogate birth and adoption.

"Go clean up, get all that snot off your face," Eva teased, knowing she must look like a blotchy mess herself.

Lacy took off for the master bathroom, smiling through glassy eyes. Eva glanced at Joe, who stood quietly and patiently by the bookcase, taking it all in. "I should clean up some, too," she said.

"Should I leave?" was his one question.

Raw from everything that had just transpired, she was honest. "I wish you wouldn't."

Chapter Ten

Eva brought two glasses of wine from the kitchen, one for Joe waiting in the living room on the couch.

"If I ever needed a glass of wine, it's now," she said, putting them on the coffee table, then plopping next to him. "Wasn't the cake delicious?"

He scraped the rest of the icing and a few crumbs from the plate and stuck the fork tines into his mouth, pulling it out clean through closed lips. "Never thought I'd enjoy pink frosting and unicorns so much."

"Glad to share." She grinned, and it felt good after the emotional hour she'd just spent with Lacy. And Joe. And her mother. "It's a girl thing, and men miss out."

"Unicorns?" He shrugged, seeming to understand,

or at least accept, the difference between men and women on their preference for unicorns, obviously okay about it. If Joe hadn't been here, would Lacy have left? She'd hate to think Lacy would've denied herself to comfort Eva. But Joe had volunteered to stay with her. The thought made her appreciate how this man had blown into her life like a whirlwind and continued to hang around like a refreshing breeze. If she couldn't trust her sister's endorsement of him, she'd be beyond help.

"I'm glad you're here," she said from her heart, taking his plate, putting it on the coffee table and replacing it with the blended red wine.

"Me, too." He'd obviously picked up on the new direction between them, and by his thoughtful expression, he was probably considering the ramifications. The lawyer ever on the job. Or was it the diplomatic mayor treading lightly and evaluating the outcome. Whatever. She was clearly overthinking her small step closer to him. Now he smiled and touched her hand, the warmth spreading up her arm. They sipped at the same time, eyes on each other, until he made a sour face.

"Wine and cake don't mix," he said, standing, gathering his plate and heading toward the kitchen. "Need some water to clear my palate."

Relaxed from her good, cleansing cry with Lacy, Eva smiled at Joe's reaction and laid her head back on the couch cushions. She really was glad he was here.

A few seconds later he returned with more than water. "Look what I found," he said, putting a plate down with a couple of leftover spring rolls from the takeout he'd brought earlier. The three had eaten before the historic phone call, and riddled with nerves, Eva had only picked at the food. Now she was hungry.

She reached for one and took a big bite before he sat. "Never knew adoption info gathering could be so draining. I'm famished."

"That's because you hardly ate dinner." So he'd noticed. Would his natural perception also pick up on her change in attitude toward him? He followed suit and popped a whole one into his mouth, then they both enjoyed their wine side by side, thighs and shoulders in full contact. His tangy aftershave mixed with the heavy red wine scent and the pork and soy sauce. His deltoid solid like a rock against her shoulder. A heady combination.

"I once ate my way through Europe after a bad breakup," she said, open and free with Joe, surprising herself.

"Yeah? Well, I once took the bar exam completely out of spite after a bad breakup."

She studied Joe in a new light; he did the same with her as another layer got lifted between them. In two sentences, they'd just said a lot about their past relationships and how they still hung them up.

"What do you say we leave that old baggage in the trash," he continued.

"Start fresh?"

He nodded, and since they'd been able to reboot to the start of their dating, she believed unloading the past once and for all was possible, too.

What a novel idea, and Joe could be the one to do it with. Maybe with him, anything could be possible. A dangerous but extremely appealing thought. He had all the traits of a great guy, further proving it with his suggestion. He had Lacy and Zack's political endorsement. He wasn't pushing her for a repeat performance of their initial crazed-sex night. In fact, he'd been the perfect gentleman ever since.

He sat beside her, glass of wine in hand, looking completely content just to be with her. Putting her under no pressure whatsoever. The sight, maybe along with the wine and the sugar high from a second piece of birthday cake she'd had earlier, completely turned her on.

"Feel like watching TV?" he asked innocently, leaning toward the remote. He really was something.

"Nope," she said, putting her glass on the table and reaching for Joe's face.

She cupped her hands on both sides of his jaw and brought his mouth to hers, kissing him with intent. Let's-get-down-to-business kind of intent. The immediate frisson thrilled her. His hands soon found her torso and pulled her closer as they kissed deeply, smashing her breasts to him. Her excitement rose as his solid chest pressed against her and his mouth ex-

plored her neck. Tingles tiptoed from every point of
contact and then across her body. Yes, this was what
she needed after the emotionally draining phone call,
a way to forget everything. Just forget. Except for
how it felt to be with Joe.

The kisses quickly got reckless, their mouths soon
searching for any bare patch of skin to latch onto.
His shirt and her top rapidly got removed and tossed,
puddled and forgotten on the floor. She'd missed his
mouth since kissing under the hibiscus. It seemed
like ages ago. Her thoughts were disintegrating and
soon only sensations remained. She'd also missed his
smooth, light brown skin, his natural scent, and from
the way he was carrying on, he'd obviously missed
her. In a repeat performance from their first night,
she found herself straddling him on the sofa. The
closer the better. But why let the confines of a couch
hold them back when, instead of being cooped up
in a limo, she had a full-size bed in the guest room?

She hopped off him and curled her finger for him
to follow, which he did with enthusiasm, as she led
him down the hall, tiptoeing past Noah's alcove—
where her boy slept in cherubic bliss—to the second
door on the left. Her home-away-from-home bedroom.

Before she opened it, a shred of conscience broke
through, and she turned to Joe. "I'm not forcing you
into doing anything you're not ready—"

His eager mouth clamped down on hers before

she could finish the sentence, and their tongues tangled in complete agreement.

The next morning, after another incredible night with Eva, Joe sneaked out the back door. Like a thief, he skulked through the neighbor's backyard to his, as early sunlight peeked through the sycamore leaves. Thanks to folks preferring yard sprawl instead of fences in Little River Valley, he'd avoided the front sidewalk. The last thing he wanted was some crazed Kitty Mittens devotee snapping his picture as he left the twins' house disheveled and unshaven. The suspicious feeling in his gut wouldn't put it past Louella Barnstable in her quest for dirt and bad press for the mayor.

As he showered, his thoughts went directly to Eva. He liked everything about her, not just her body, but everything else, too, including the fact she'd adopted a baby on her own. She was independent, unlike the other rich girls he'd known, especially Victoria, who'd never worked a day in her life. And determined, with goals and achievements to back up her dreams. Dreams Come True popped into his mind, forcing an ironic thought. Had he been dreaming about something he wasn't even aware of before he met Eva?

The last thing he'd wanted this morning was to leave Eva's warm, supple body in bed, alone, but Monday was a big day at the front end of an even bigger week. He had an interview scheduled with the *Little River Valley Voice* at nine, Zack's senior living model home opening at one, and a mayoral meeting with the school board at three. Tuesday was booked similarly, and Wednesday night, there was a fund-raiser at Olive, the chic wine and appetizer bar in midtown. Supporters were paying a couple hundred bucks to pop shrimp puffs and drink organic designer wine to help his campaign in the last weeks of the election.

While drying off, he snapped his fingers at his first mistake of the day, having forgotten to invite Eva for Wednesday's affair.

Truth was, he'd been a bit gun-shy with her, not solely because of the election, but also because of who she was. How many times did he need to make the same mistake? Taking a woman's interest and assuming it meant more, as in, "you're good enough."

Victoria hadn't been the only mistake of his dating life, just the hardest to take. Time and again he'd let himself get involved with women who didn't have a clue what it was like to be a farm worker's kid. Even the Latinas he'd dated had come from middle-class homes and knew nothing about true poverty and the constant battle to survive growing up. He may have worn thrift store clothes, but they were always clean and pressed by his abuela.

He'd come from nothing, literally nothing, materially, that is, but his parents and his abuela had taught him how to enjoy life and take the challenges as just that, something to overcome. He'd made it over so many hurdles in life, beginning in kindergarten with English immersion and becoming the first in his family to graduate from high school.

He'd suffered rebuffs from what seemed like more than his share of girls along the way. Not when it was just him and them, but always when it came time to meet their families. That was when the veil was lifted, and they fell out of infatuation with him. When he'd turned out to not measure up to the parents' expectations, as if he was a gangbanger or something. The one thing his father would've kicked his butt over.

Then, to his family's amazement, he continued on through undergraduate school to law school. He'd had to beg and borrow, but he had never stolen a penny. Now he was strapped with debt, but proud to be a productive citizen.

Yet deep down he still felt that maybe he wasn't good enough. Maybe he'd forgotten to invite Eva to the party because he wanted to put off that moment when her vision would come into focus.

Ridiculous in this day and age or not, Joe's expectations were based on personal experience. To some people he'd never measure up.

He rubbed the towel over his head, still planning to call her after the interview to ask her to be his date. It wasn't the smartest thing to do campaign-wise, but he needed to test her. If she was going to change her mind about him, he'd rather know sooner than later. Despite the doubt and his personal dating history to reinforce it, he still wanted to run right back to her bed and forget about everything else.

Sitting in the naturally lit—thanks to a skylight—and cramped mayor's office in the tiny city hall of LRV, Joe gave the journalist his full attention.

So far the newspaper interview had gone as expected, with questions about his education, his law practice and what it was like being mayor. She'd just finished asking him about Louella Barnstable, and he'd given his most diplomatic and rehearsed reply, praising her for running for office. Now the young female was taking a different angle.

"Tell us about Savannah Schuster, your number one senior citizen supporter?"

He couldn't hide the smile. "She's a great lady."

"She seems to be on the opposite side of most of the Change the Charter movement."

"Weren't you at the rally Saturday? I announced after negotiations that half the food establishments in town will be offering breakfast discounts to seniors. I consider that the perfect compromise to changing a charter drafted by the founders of Little River Valley. Think I won over more than my share of seniors, too."

"Well, the latest polls aren't out yet." She tapped

her lip with an old-school #2 pencil eraser. "There are those who say letting in fast-food chains will create jobs, and many seniors need to work part-time to make ends meet."

So it isn't solely about their stomachs and pocketbooks. Right. "There are plenty of small businesses in town looking for part-time help. I see posters in windows every time I walk down Main Street." He wasn't going any further down this path, which led to Louella and her crew.

"Back to Savannah," he said. "As you know from the article your paper ran, I met her when Dreams Come True arranged her wish, which included having dinner with me." He gave his politician smile, assuming he'd answered the prior question adequately without losing his cool and was ready to move on.

"Is that where you met—" the journalist glanced at her small notepad for reference "—Evangelina Taylor DeLongpre?"

He tensed, and warmth sprung near his collar. Where was she going with this? Forcing an unfazed expression, he went succinct. "Yes."

And that was all she was getting out of him on the topic of Eva. A topic he could fixate on for hours and hours and still not figure out. Or how he could go on for days about her appeal and charms and, oh yeah, how perfectly they fit together. Including how fantastic they made each other feel. The warmth turned to heat on his neck. If he didn't watch out, he'd get sweaty in no time, especially with the flash of flesh from last night suddenly whirling through his tense thoughts. He needed to be on his toes, and instead he slid to sweet and hot memories from last night, to avoid being on the hot seat.

The journalist glanced again at her notes. "She has a son?"

"Is this relevant to our interview?"

At first she looked uncomfortable, but soon sneaky determination invaded her fresh-out-of-college eyes. "Well, we, the public, cannot help but notice how much the baby looks like you."

Putting the diplomatic mayor aside, he went directly into lawyer mode. "Are you implying that because her son is Hispanic, like me, that there is somehow a connection?" He didn't give her a chance to respond. "Because if you are, be careful to not make a generalization."

Her eyes went wide. "Not at all what I meant, Mayor Aguirre. My apologies."

Oh, really? Who knew what her true response was, if she really was sorry, or what her intentions were by asking about Noah, but he was not going there.

"Is there anything else you'd like to talk about," he said, taking back control of this interview. "For instance, the senior living model home opening today? A new development that will help a hundred seniors find comfort and convenience in Little River Valley, thanks to my approving the project last year?"

"Oh yes, we'll be there covering it."

"Great. See you, then, and my thanks to the *Little River Valley Voice* for its support of me in the last election and since becoming mayor." Though he still hadn't been given the newspaper's endorsement this time around.

They shook hands; hers was cold and limp. He'd had a lot of experience with handshakes and he never trusted the floppy ones. Without further questions, the young journalist gathered her things and quietly left his office, muttering her thanks before closing the door.

Later, as planned, Joe arrived at Zack Gardner's construction site. What had once been a huge dirt-and-rocks lot had undergone a metamorphosis into a circle of bright little cottages on a neatly manicured street. People milled around on the sidewalks, pamphlets in their hands, checking out the numbers of each of three model houses. They ranged from a tiny one-bedroom at 900 square feet, to a second larger cottage with a slightly bigger single bedroom, to a spacious two-moderate-sized-bedroom cottage, measuring 1,200 square feet.

Heading for the main clubhouse, where security and a small gym and recreation room were housed and where the event was set to be held, Joe walked through the good-sized crowd to find Zack.

Lacy was at his side, and next to Lacy was Eva. His heart tripped and his outlook brightened at the sight of Eva until he saw the same journalist from that morning nearby. Eva had Noah on her hip and was standing next to Savannah. From far across the room, he subtly took out his phone and texted her.

Can't hang out with you. I'll explain later.

Shaking hands through the crowd, he surreptitiously watched as she retrieved her phone and read the text. Her brows came together. She didn't look happy. Nothing he could do about it now. But dang.

Dark-blond-haired, long-legged Zack strode across the room, out of character in a suit and tie instead of work boots and jeans, a huge grin on his face. "There's the man. I mean the mayor," Zack said loudly as he threw out his hand. Joe slapped his palm into his friend's and they shook hands like the long-term buddies they were. Now theirs was a handshake.

"This place looks amazing. You've done great work." Joe had been so busy he hadn't been by the construction site in over a month. Not since meeting Eva.

"All thanks to you giving me the green light."

"What's good for our seniors is good for our community," Joe let a totally political-sounding phrase slip, though he wholeheartedly believed it.

"Can you smile for the newspaper, please?"

Joe recognized the voice, having spent part of his morning with her. He and Zack turned their heads and posed in the middle of a handshake for the photographer as the reporter approached. All he could hope was the newspaper might quote him on that perfect sound bite. Zack was ready for her questions and gladly answered each one. While he did, Joe peeked across the way to see Lacy and Eva talking with several white-haired guests.

After the brief interview with the contractor and mayor, the time came for Joe to make his public congratulations and give a pep talk about the project. Once through his first couple of sentences, Noah started fussing and crying. Lacy took him from Eva as Joe continued his speech, but the baby would have nothing to do with her, either. Noah turned and squealed, reaching out, pumping his legs in frustration when Joe didn't respond. Eva took Noah back and headed for the exit while Noah cried, "Da! Da!" loudly, still reaching out to where Joe stood. "Daaah!"

He'd never done that before.

The incident drew the interest of the journalist, who watched the fussy baby, Da-Da sounds and all. Her suspicious gaze slowly returned to Joe as she made a quick notation on her small pad.

"Hey, I'm sure you folks didn't come here to hear me talk," Joe said. "So without further waiting, let's take a tour of the beautiful cottages."

Eva was nowhere in sight when they stepped outside into the sunny and cool day onto the new street, which looked perfect as a movie set. In the distance he still heard Noah, who was not a happy camper.

After the tour, once the newspaper crew had left, Joe looked for Eva. She was under a tree, where Lacy had set up her pink food truck and was serving her specialty of home-baked hand pies and coffee to all the guests. Feeling safe, Joe started toward Eva, and Noah went into his reaching act again.

"Sorry," she said, looking flustered, "I couldn't control him."

"Nothing to be sorry about," Joe said, taking one last quick look around before taking Noah from Eva. "Hey, buds, what was up with that?"

"Da!" Noah kicked his feet and grinned.

An odd sensation came over Joe. How would it feel to be married and have this kid as his son, a baby boy who clearly worshipped him? Joe gave Noah a kiss on his chubby and sticky cheek.

"If anyone should be apologizing, it should be me for the text I had to send." He lowered his voice. "The interview this morning got weird. The journalist started asking about you and Noah, like somehow I was his father or something."

Down went Eva's brows. "That's not good. Why do they keep assuming such a thing?"

"Look at us."

She studied her son, with Joe still holding him. "Well, only the color of your hair and eyes, but that's it."

"And I definitely don't have his pot belly," Joe teased, tickling Noah's.

"There you go. Absolutely no resemblance. At all."

It felt good to lighten up and chuckle together. Noah had obviously brightened up, too. He'd hated when they'd had to ignore each other, especially when Noah busted them with his tears and cries of "Da! Da!" What would little Miss Journalist do with that?

He glanced around at all the silver foxes and maidens. Some of them looked familiar, like he'd seen them at the rallies—holding signs and chanting, "Change the Charter." His stomach clenched. What if one of them was Kitty Mittens and here he was with Eva, holding her son. His jaw clenched.

"What's the matter?"

"I'm getting paranoid about that Facebook page."

"Here, let me have him," Eva said, seeming to read his mind. Though Joe sensed frustration in her tone.

"I'm sorry. You know this is the last way I want to be around you." He moved closer to her ear. "Just remember last night." Only then did he notice a little lady in purple, wearing a red hat, standing within earshot, canting her head in their direction. It wasn't Louella, but who knew who she was or what she'd heard.

Man, some days he hated being a public figure. He made a snap decision not to let it get in his way. "Oh, hey, I didn't get the chance to ask you earlier."

"When we were otherwise engaged?" Eva said, flirting for the first time that day, taunting him with her deviously sexy look. She remembered everything, just like he did. Wow.

"Uh, yeah." There went the warm collar bit again. "So, anyway. Will you be my date at the function at Olive on Wednesday night?"

"The fund-raiser?"

"Yes. The press isn't invited."

She stood perfectly still, considering his offer. Noah grabbed Joe's ear and yanked while they waited. Joe blew Noah a raspberry, which made the little fellow laugh, so he did it again. After a few seconds, Eva gave a measured look.

"Sorry, I'm babysitting."

All they'd overcome in the past week seemed to disappear with those three little words.

Chapter Eleven

Wednesday night being a school night, Eva had gone to Zack's house to watch Emma so he and Lacy could attend the fund-raiser. She'd set up the travel play-and-sleep bed for Noah in a guest room, and by 9:00 p.m. both Emma and Noah were asleep.

She walked throughout the completely remodeled California ranch house. The modern yet homey place had great bones, and she could see Lacy living here. Lacy had found a man to love and a small ready-made family with Emma, who clearly adored her stepmother-to-be.

The thought of that inevitable move made her wonder what would happen to Lacy's house. It carried the history of John Winters, the father she'd never had the chance to know. Did it matter? History couldn't be changed, and hanging on to a house that had never factored into Eva's life until recently made no sense on the logical side. Yet, the truth was, it would matter to Eva. Maybe she'd buy it?

And live practically next door to Joe?

Why wasn't it possible to keep him out of her mind for fifteen minutes? Was that asking too much? The man had a way of sneaking into her thoughts and holding her hostage at the oddest times. Like right now. Usually, nothing distracted her while working on Dreams Come True business, but thanks to Savannah's wish, all that had changed. There was no peace. No hiding place. She'd met a man that knocked her world sideways on every level, yet they were stuck in a holding pattern.

She wished she could've been his date at Olive tonight but had thought it best not to be seen with him in public, even though it was a private function. Who knew who might be there? Besides, she'd already agreed to babysit Emma for Zack before Joe had gotten around to asking. Two days' notice seemed a bit like being taken for granted anyway. Already? Seriously. And Lacy would finally have a chance to wear that peacock dress she'd been drooling over since the try-on session the day of the fateful Dreams Come True dinner date with Joe. Lacy looked fabu-

lous in it, too, and Zack couldn't keep his eyes off
her before they'd left.

The house was quiet; she'd finished the one sit-
com she liked. With dozens of choices on TV, after
scrolling through no less than twenty channels, she
had no interest in watching anything else. At eleven,
she drifted to the updated kitchen, a warm and welcoming place, to make some herbal tea. As she sat at
the modern island and waited for the water to boil,
she saw the local paper on the opposite counter, still
unrolled inside a rubber band, and took it to where
she sat.

Having brewed some vanilla chamomile, Eva
sipped her tea, looked around the kitchen and out to
the fabulous deck, and smiled. She was glad to see
her sister happy, after so many years of grieving over
the loss of everyone she'd loved. Eva took another
sip, the subtle, sweet scent of the tea steam wafting
up her nose, and then smiled wider. Once Lacy had
fallen in love with Zack, she'd found Eva, and life
just kept getting better.

On that upbeat note, she removed the rubber band
from the paper and opened it to peruse while she finished her tea. In a nice surprise, page one had a great
picture of Joe next to the interview that had caused
him to send that warning text at the model home
opening on Monday. The title quoted his bumper
sticker slogan: Locally Grown, Promising to Keep
Little River Valley Sustainable. She read on with

caution but was beyond happy to note it was a solid article about his time as mayor of Little River Valley. Including his accomplishments and aspirations for the city's future. Sure, the author brought up Louella Barnstable but fairly stated that Louella's concerns about cost-friendly breakfasts for seniors had been addressed in a way that didn't need a change to the charter.

Page two made Eva inhale and nearly choke on what was left of the tea. There she was with Noah on her hip, standing next to Joe at the model home opening. The picture caption said, "Mayor Aguirre with special supporter Eva DeLongpre and son." Hadn't the reporter left by that time?

Clearly glad she hadn't gone with Joe tonight, when further evidence pictures would surely have been taken surreptitiously, she read on.

After subtly insinuating there was something going on between her and Joe, with the "special" status beside her name, the second part of the article brought up other questions Louella had. True, they weren't about her and Joe's relationship, but concerns on how the current mayor used the argument that balancing the city budget was top of his list, when he still had huge personal debt from outstanding school loans.

Wasn't that the story with just about everyone who'd attained a postgrad degree?

Eva pulled in her chin. What a slap in the face to

Joe. But then again, Louella was from her mother's era and had a different way of seeing things. Pay as you go was her mother's theme song. She'd taught Eva early on how to budget. Her mother had made something out of herself from hard work and counting pennies. Eva was expected to never forget that, and to not take her wealth for granted. But most of her generation had had to take out loans for higher education. Louella's voiced concerns might fall on a lot of deaf ears. Still, Eva wondered how anyone had dug up such private information about Joe? It seemed underhanded, a dirty tactic. Yet...

How much does *he owe?*

Oh no, that was probably the question with which every other reader of this article was left. And the answer wasn't any more her business than theirs.

She dropped her head in her hands. Why did anyone ever want to run for public office when their personal lives got turned inside out for everyone to pick apart at will?

The front door opened. Eva closed the paper and rushed to the front room. Zack and Lacy looked like a power couple dressed for the Oscars and were standing in the entryway smiling and chatting. The door wasn't closed all the way, and a brisk breeze came through.

Eva rubbed her arms to warm them. "Hi," she said, unable to hide her happiness for Lacy. "Have a good time, kids?"

"I haven't felt this grown up in ages," Lacy said, Zack taking her wrap and kissing her neck before hanging it on the coatrack.

The front door swung wide and in stepped Joe in a blast of night air, wearing a basic black tuxedo and looking *GQ* gorgeous. Her heart nearly stopped at the sight. How could he do that to her, by just showing up?

"Hi," he said, his eyes dancing over her as though she was in a nightgown instead of yoga pants and a fitting top. "I'm your ride home."

This was news to her. She and Lacy had driven to Zack's together, and she assumed she'd take the car home.

"I've got an early appointment tomorrow," Lacy was quick to point out.

Was this a preplanned scheme to give Eva time alone with Joe? May as well throw a bucket of water on it. "Have you seen the article in the paper?" she blurted.

Joe's brows lifted as he nodded and stuck hands in his pockets. "Oh yes."

"What article?" Zack asked, finally tearing his gaze from her sister.

"It was in today's *Voice*. I just found it on your kitchen counter."

"Bad news?" Lacy asked, her prior dreamy expression turning to concern.

Joe sighed. "They somehow found out I still owe

on my student loans from law school. It's not like I'm not paying them down, I just haven't paid them off yet."

"I've heard law school costs almost as much as med school," Zack added.

"I went to Stanford," Joe said with an I-rest-my-case glance.

Eva had let the article get to her and she'd even felt a little annoyed with Joe because of it but being face-to-face with him seemed to change everything. All she wanted to do was be supportive. "It still doesn't seem relevant to being mayor," Eva said.

"Does to Louella Barnstable" was all Joe said. "You ready for your ride home?"

They dropped the subject, said their goodbyes, and Eva picked up Noah with Joe's help, gathering all the necessary bags and blankets. On the drive she focused on having Joe all to herself, enjoying the dressed-up version, including a sharp, expensive-smelling cologne. Noah slept soundly in his car seat in the back, the situation feeling far too close to being a family. Sudden concern for Joe surprised her.

"I hope you don't mind my asking, but are you in debt, Joe?"

"I still owe a lot, but not nearly as much as I used to. Back then I had something to prove, and I could've gone to a far less expensive law school. Pride and, I won't lie, the status kept me from turning down Stanford when they accepted me. Now I'm still paying for it and will for a long time to come. What about you?" He glanced at her—his expression revealed realization mixed with disappointment.

"Mom paid for everything." Her mother hadn't inherited anything, unlike her, and it had been a big deal to Bridget to afford a master's degree for Eva. She focused on pride for her mother instead of the twinge of guilt that wanted to spring up.

He shook his head as if there was no way she could understand. She'd known they'd come from different backgrounds, but right now he made her feel like it was different worlds.

"What did you have to prove?" She saw a man equal to her on every level, nothing more.

"That I was as good as everyone else."

"Why?" Lame, obvious question or not, she wanted to know.

He started a long reply in Spanish which started with *mi hijo* and went on from there. Her Spanish was elementary at best and she struggled to understand. After making his point, or working through his frustration, she wasn't sure which was his main point, he switched to English. "People have a way of making others feel unworthy. Do I need to spell it out for you? I didn't speak English when I started school, I dressed differently, I ate differently. As I assimilated, I still felt different, and there were plenty of people ready and willing to make sure I did."

The admission crushed her. She'd grown up taking for granted what Joe's family had struggled for his entire life. "But your parents knew you were good enough, and you've proved them right. You're a mayor now. A lawyer. Who had the nerve to tell you to your face you weren't good enough?"

He took a breath, tension turning his lips into a straight line as he let it out and thought. "The woman I fell in love with during my undergraduate studies."

Though her heart stung for him, she moderated her response. "Ah, that baggage we're both throwing out."

"Yeah, except mine came with a literal price tag."

"But not the big prize."

"Nope, she married a rich guy, like her. But I've got a law degree and as you said, I'm a sitting mayor."

"More important, you're a remarkable person. I'm honored to know you."

She reached across and caressed his arm; he let go of the steering wheel, driving with one hand to hold hers. As they glanced at each other, she felt something special connected them. He'd shared an old and lifelong hurt, making himself vulnerable, because he trusted her. She never wanted to let him down.

When they got to the house, Joe brought Noah, snug in his carrier, as Eva unlocked and opened the door. Admittedly, she was paranoid someone might be watching. After putting her son in his home-away-from-home bed, a used crib they'd found at a second-hand store in downtown Little River Valley, she went to find Joe. Instead of sitting on the couch waiting for her to rush into his arms, he stood by the front door.

Ready to convince him to stay, she put her arms around his neck and kissed him. His hands went to her hips, and as their kisses heated up, he walked her a few small steps backward to the entry wall. She rested against it as he took his time to nip at her ear and neck, making her sigh and tense at the same time. His fingers lightly traveled across her body, tickling, teasing, firing her up. She dropped her hold to lace her arms around his torso and brought him closer. He smelled so good and tasted even better, and all she could think was more, more and more. Balanced against the wall, she lifted one leg, wrapping it around his hip, in close contact, exactly where she wanted. Their kissing never stopped until he broke free.

"Wish I could stay."

"You can!" How had she become so easy where Joe was concerned?

"No. I can't. Mike has me speaking at the Chamber of Commerce breakfast at six thirty tomorrow. If I stay here, and do everything I want to with you, I won't get any sleep, and I need to be coherent by six."

She couldn't help her groan. "When?"

"When what?" he said, studying her body, obviously still lost in the feel of her.

"Will you do all the things you want to, to me?"

A devilish smile brightened his prior dark bedroom gaze. "Friday? My house? Can Lacy babysit Noah?"

Even in the heat of their moment, he thought about Noah. Her boy wasn't an obstacle to get around, but a part of who she was, and he clearly liked and accepted it, always treating her son with care. "I'll beg her."

They kissed again, an obvious "last call" taste of each other. With her body alive and dancing in anticipation, but with nowhere to follow up, she'd have to do some intense yoga to calm back down once he left.

"See you Friday, then," he said, regrettably letting her go.

Good thing she had the wall to prop against, since her legs had gone wobbly under his touch. There was something important she wanted to tell him, but her mind was foggy because of him.

"Good night," he said, reaching for the handle, opening the door.

"Good night." With it closed, she listened to his footsteps down the porch as the air cleared of his spell and she slowly remembered what she'd wanted to tell him. *You don't have to prove anything to me. I know all I need to know.*

As Joe undressed, hanging up the tux he'd bought when he'd first been elected mayor, he went over the conversation with Eva in the car. He'd never told a woman about his insecurities growing up. He'd always preferred to go the macho route, suppress those old and ugly feelings, then act overconfident to compensate.

When his original prom date backed out last minute, presumably because her daddy didn't approve, he asked two friends, girls who didn't have dates to the prom, and walked in with a girl on each arm and a broad grin. Only Miguel suspected how he really felt.

When Victoria gutted him, ripping away his American dream, he came up with a new one. Work for the people as a lawyer and why the hell not run for mayor?

But he'd just spent the better part of the drive home telling Eva how he'd really felt for most of his life, how those negative thoughts could still invade his mind. His baggage.

The baggage Eva had called him out on, only had power over him if he let it.

He loosened his tie. He'd shown her who he really was, and her reply had been that she was honored to know him. This from a smart woman with good taste. Maybe it was time to dump the garbage and believe Eva. He deserved everything he'd worked for, even a woman like Eva.

When he stripped down to his boxers, he never felt freer in his life.

Thursday night, they all attended the mayoral debate, including Zack, Lacy, Noah and Savannah, whom Eva had brought. Joe took the diplomatic approach, but Louella Barnstable had come with her guns fully loaded. Eva couldn't believe how ruthless the little silver-haired woman with the Tyrolean plait could be.

Her opening comments were lofty, promising the moon. Joe came off practical and competent.

"I do not have a love child," Joe calmly responded when later in the debate she'd insinuated so with her first lie.

"Yes, I still have law school loans, but I am paying them off, not reneging on them as many others have," he said, when she'd insisted he couldn't balance a city budget if he was personally in debt.

Then…

"Not true," he countered when she'd so much as accused him of misuse of position and use of government property. "I have a separate office for my law practice, which I use for reelection purposes, not city hall."

And a half hour later, during Louella's closing statements, listeners would think Little River Valley would spontaneously combust if Joe Aguirre got reelected. Her final remarks were delivered with fiery words and fisted gestures. While Joe, when it was his turn, plainly and calmly stated what he planned to do to keep their community both family- and small business–friendly, while meeting the needs of their growing senior population and natural city growth.

Eva cupped hands around her mouth. "Woo-hoo!" Loud applause in the auditorium continued for a full minute when the debate ended. Hopefully, most would be voting for Joe, but who knew? There hadn't been any recent polls.

Sitting a few rows back, on the end in case she needed a quick getaway with Noah acting up, Eva sprang to her feet, and with Savannah by her side, approached the stage at the end. Her first mistake was kissing Joe's cheek; her second was letting him take Noah off her hands, the kid clearly loving being in his arms. Lights snapped from cameras all around. When a local TV station reporter stepped toward Joe with a microphone, Eva moved back, pulling Savannah with her, before being able to retrieve Noah from Joe. Mistake number three.

Talk about feeding the secret love child fire!

Later, Eva delivered Savannah safely home—her newest friend happily talking about what a great debate Joe had had the entire drive. They said their good-nights and hugged, and Eva felt in a small way she'd found a surrogate grandma. Even Nipsey was getting used to Eva and had quit barking every time she stepped inside Savannah's apartment. With happy thoughts, she returned to Zack's house, where they all waited for her so they could share a toast.

Joe was relieved to have the one and only debate behind him, and happy to see Eva walk through the door. He went to her and returned the kiss on the cheek she'd given him earlier, when he'd been unable to respond publicly.

"So what is it with you two," Zack said, holding an empty glass and waiting for the pour, a mischievous twinkle in his green eyes. "Is there something the good people of Little River Valley should know?"

Joe left his arm around Eva's waist, but kept his thoughts to himself, offering a noncommittal smile. These were Eva's people and he'd respect her wishes whether to tell or not.

"That we're bonking each other's brains out?" Eva let fly as Lacy gasped, nearly dropping the champagne bottle. "Seriously, Lacy, you didn't know?" She gave Joe a straight-on stare and batted her lashes. "Someone needs to let Kitty Mittens, Feline at Large, in on our secret for the sake of the city."

Joe laughed, then pulled her hip closer to his, having never expected Eva to be so daring and verbal about their relationship, and kissed her the way he'd really wanted when she'd arrived. Which turned into a longer and more involved kiss than he'd expected, thanks to the heat of the moment and Eva's bold announcement. Yes, they were "bonking," thank you very much, every chance they got! Which wasn't nearly enough, in his book.

Zack dipped his head, giving Joe and Eva some privacy while they engaged in extreme PDA. Joe liked coming clean with his friends. He and Eva had nothing to hide. In fact, after their conversation in the car and her response to his confession, a little voice kept nagging that she might be the one.

His cell went off, and he ended the kiss with regret, assuming it would be Mike. Who else? He answered only to hear a string of curses in Spanish. Talk about mood breaker. They hadn't even toasted yet.

"Wait, wait, wait. Slow down."

"This is not good."

"What's not good?"

Joe's text pinged with Mike's annoying digital ringtone. "Check it out."

A picture popped up. The one where Joe stood at Lacy's window comforting Noah the night he'd been teething. A sinking sensation slid through his stomach as he read the caption. "Love child? Or overattentive surrogate dad?" He groaned.

"What is it?" Eva rushed to his side and immediately saw what he was staring at. She sucked in a short, strangled sound.

Then Lacy and Zack scrambled over and looked. "When did that happen?" Lacy was first to ask.

"That Wednesday you made dinner for us," Eva said, defeated. She grabbed Joe's arm and squeezed, her clutch not the least bit consoling. "And then went to Zack's."

"Well," he said, resigned, "Louella will have a field day with this."

"And people will indulge in their favorite pastime and jump to conclusions," Zack said, uncharacteristically cynical.

Joe sighed. "I've got to believe most will do their homework and blow this off. I was just a man trying to help a baby calm down."

"While I set out dinner. Like a private family," Eva said, beginning to sound angry. "You deserve your privacy! What makes them think they can sneak around and stalk you and expose your private life?" She'd quickly escalated to irate.

Joe took her hand and squeezed. "We can't do anything about this right now, and we came here to celebrate. Lacy? You gonna open that bottle and share or what?"

As his father warned him when he first decided to run for mayor, *más vale saber encajar los golpes*. You'd better be able to roll with the punches.

"Not much we can do about this anyway, so let's drink." He forced a well-practiced confident smile, not feeling it in the least. Refusing to let lies get him down, he remembered the solid debate and by the time Zack had popped the cork, his smile had circled around to feeling genuine.

After Lacy poured the bubbly, Zack raised his glass. "To a great debate. The rest is all BS."

They shared a relieving group laugh and drank their glasses down, then Lacy poured another round for the guys.

* * *

On Friday night Joe and Eva finally had time alone together at his house. They'd dealt with and shelved the ongoing fake and misleading reports on social media. Of Kitty Mittens's 2K followers, most, it seemed, didn't live in Little River Valley, since Joe insisted there hadn't been any calls coming to his office/headquarters about the picture. Mike had reported a couple of hotheads, but they were clearly not voting for Joe anyway, secret baby or not.

She'd put Noah to bed first, and Lacy promised to babysit, since Zack was coming to their house. Now, alone at last, Joe and Eva said hello. They kissed, and Joe walked backward down the hall as they continued to kiss and grope, immediately falling onto his bed and stripping each other clean. It seemed like forever since they'd been together. Within minutes of driving her crazy with kisses and touches, he reached for the new stash of condoms he kept beside his bed since meeting Eva, then tilted his head as though a thought had just occurred.

"We're good, right?" He held up the foil packet.

The idea of birth control stopped her cold. Their first time together had been completely spontaneous, but since realizing they might be having repeat performances, she'd gone on the pill as soon as she could, but starting any old time in the cycle meant no coverage for seven days. They'd been depending on Joe.

"Seems like you'd have your period by now?" he added.

When was my last period?

As anxiety built, more thoughts occurred. Maybe the pills threw this month off. Then more thoughts. How was it he'd noticed the time lapse and she hadn't? She'd always been completely responsible when it came to such things. Yet this time around, she'd been...well, not herself. Ditzy even. Completely out of character. But Joe had a way of doing that to her. And he'd always used a condom, even that first night when he'd had to fish one out of his wallet that looked like it had been there for years and worse for the wear. At least it was something.

Another shot of adrenaline let go across her chest. It could've been long past its expiration date. In the heat of the moment, they certainly hadn't bothered to check.

A deep chill cut through her center. "You're right," she said, her voice quivery. "I'm late!"

Chapter Twelve

"We better check right now," Joe said, sitting bolt upright on his bed. The dark room felt suddenly oppressive and cold.

Eva and Joe jumped off the bed and got dressed in record time. They drove in dreaded silence to the local pharmacy to buy a kit. When Joe parked, Eva reached over and stopped him before he got out.

"You can't go in with me. Not when I'm buying a pregnancy test. Who knows where Kitty Mittens has eyes?" Damn feline at large.

"Don't be paranoid."

She clenched his forearm. "Joe, you're a public figure around here, running for reelection. This is what is known as a scandal. The timing couldn't be worse. Stay here."

She pulled the hood up on her beach-glass-blue-colored sweatshirt, tucking inside as much of her red hair as possible. She opened her purse and started to slip on her sunglasses, when Joe took her hand. She glanced up at him shaking his head.

"Too much," he said, kindly.

Feeling more like someone planning a heist than buying a kit, she opened the door.

"Wait," he said, digging out his wallet and handing her money. "The least I can do is pay for it."

She cringed inside. In the long run, they might both pay for it.

She slunk inside the pharmacy and found the aisle where the kits were kept, then bought the digital one that said it could detect early pregnancies. Never in her life had she expected to be in this situation, and as she paid, a lump formed in her throat. She tried her best to keep from crying in public. She made it through the transaction by avoiding eye contact, but on her way back to the car, her chin quivered, and eyes brimmed. She swiped early tears aside, determined to have it together before she got back to the car.

On a deep inhale, she slipped inside the car and buckled up. "Deed done."

He nodded slowly, sympathetically, reaching for and holding her hand, his warm and hers cold from night air. "Whatever turns out, we're in this together."

Well, fact was, it was usually on the woman in this situation, but decent as ever, he'd inserted himself into it.

A few minutes later they parked in his garage and closed the door before exiting the car. This was new, and only because there were people seeming to hide in the bushes to get compromising pictures of him. Without another word, they took the test inside and Eva went directly to the bathroom, where she closed the door.

Joe was shut out from Eva as she took the pregnancy test. He paced, never having been in this situation before. One little thing that looked like a digital thermometer could rewrite both of their futures. Amazing. The thought of becoming a father forced a hundred quick thoughts. He'd met an amazing woman. They'd had a most unusual start. His determination to restart their dating clock reinforced how much he liked Eva. Even while trying to slow things down, they couldn't keep their hands off each other. *Amazing* was the word of the moment, because that was the only way he could describe their lovemaking. Truth was, he liked everything about her, and even before tonight, he could see a future with her. It all depended on her and what she wanted. Positive or negative, he was ready to take the next step. Which in itself was freaking amazing.

The bathroom door creaked open and his heart rate doubled. Eva's pale complexion and serious eyes told the story. He didn't need to hear…

"It's positive," she whispered.

"Amazing," he blurted without irony, the word pinned to his heart.

Then she cried. Which crushed him as he pulled her to his chest and she crumpled against him while he held her up. With Eva tight in his arms, he kissed the crown of her head as she sobbed, wanting her to know it was fine. Wonderful, in fact. This was how they seemed to do things, fast and out of order. But he needed to wait, to see where she was emotionally. And above all, not to push her in any direction.

"Is it the end of the world?" He'd only heard her cry with Lacy, but never wanted to be the reason.

"This wasn't in my five-year plan," she blubbered.

"It wasn't in mine, either, but here we are." Trying his best to keep his head together—which surprisingly was in a calm and collected state—for the sake of both of them.

"Noah's only just turned one!"

"True." What could he say? She was stuck on plans and unwanted surprises. Well, he could relate to that, too. But in this case the surprise seemed… just how did it seem? Awesome actually. A baby with the most amazing woman he'd ever met. "Look, I know it's early in the relationship, that we're still feeling our way around getting to know each other, but it feels right to me. I say let's go for it," he said, without thinking through the meaning of those words.

She tensed in his arms. "How very pragmatic of you."

He'd been deep in his head, figuring out his feelings about their news, hadn't thought to gauge where she might be, beyond shocked and crying.

Gazing up, she captured his eyes. "Unfortunately, that's not what I'm looking for in a proposal."

Yeah, he should've worded it better, but the true intention was there. "I understand, not very romantic, but it's sincere. I mean it. Why not?" He held her out a bit to better see her and watch her reaction. "We're crazy about each other. Well, I am, won't speak for you. We're compatible. I think about you all the time when you're not around. I haven't put a word to it yet, but…"

"Please don't say anything else. We're not in our right minds right now. We've already made a baby and I don't want to rush into anything else right this minute. I need time to deal with this." Her hand fell to her abdomen.

"I understand." He bent and kissed her tenderly, then took her hand and led her to the bedroom. She hesitated at the door.

"This never helps me think straight," she said.

"Trust me here."

After a moment's thought, Eva allowed him to

take her to his bed, undress her down to her underwear with care and consideration, and love. Yeah. The pregnancy may have forced the word out, but it was true. He wouldn't deny that he'd fallen in love with Eva.

He put her to bed and tucked the covers around her before he undressed to his briefs, then hopped in and spooned up behind her. "All I want to do is hold you."

They settled into each other, snuggling together. Slowly he sensed the tension leave her body as her breathing slowed and her head rested gently on his shoulder. Then her eyes fluttered shut.

He kissed her forehead. "Good night, *mi amor.*"

In the last twelve months, Eva had adopted a son and bought a house, moving to a new city. In the past month every other aspect of Eva's life had also changed. She'd met Joe, temporarily moved in with her sister, gotten involved with a good man. In the last twelve hours, all those prior changes seemed like nothing compared with being pregnant.

She and Joe had parted that morning with a hug and kiss. No words. He'd said all he'd needed last night. For now, their passion had been forgotten over the news of becoming parents. He was rolling toward the end of the election and had a city to run. She knew they wouldn't see each other for the next couple of days, and totally understood. She was glad, even, needing time to think without his influence over her thoughts. And she certainly had a lot to think about.

Lacy immediately knew something was up. "I hope you and Joe didn't break up because of that stupid picture."

"No. We didn't. He's super busy right now, and I've got a lot of work to catch up on, that's all."

Lacy wasn't convinced, Eva could tell, but this time, surprisingly, she didn't press, and Eva was grateful for that. It would take a while to wrap her brain around being pregnant, and she didn't want Lacy to know until she'd made peace with her situation. This was supposed to be Lacy's big time, engaged, planning a wedding. Instead Eva had materialized, taking center stage, throwing everything off track. And now this. Might Lacy resent her for overshadowing the most important time in a future bride's life?

She studied her sister, the stranger she'd shared a womb with and years later had quickly gotten to know, who didn't have a resentful bone in her body. Lacy was nosy and sometimes a little pushy, but right now she instinctively knew to step back and let things be. More importantly, Eva trusted that Lacy would be as thrilled as Eva should be about the news when she finally told her. Maybe she should start working on that part, the excitement, the joy, instead of all the practicalities.

Joe called every day and they talked. He was always upbeat, but respectful of her need to be the only one making a decision. Eva didn't want to see him, but rather focus more on being pregnant and what it all meant in the scheme of her future. Could she handle being a single mother of two? Joe had said, *Let's go for it*, but she'd never wanted to have to get married, and she'd always suspect he'd felt forced to propose if she jumped right in and said yes. Though a part of her really wanted to. There was loads to think about and not enough hours in the day to do it.

On Sunday, Lacy prepared their third birthday cake for ages eleven to fifteen. It would be their boy-crazy cake, and they planned to share all their favorite boy bands and songs that afternoon as they celebrated more of the birthdays they'd missed. It was good to have the distraction of combing her brain for those nearly forgotten memories. Not surprisingly, they'd both crushed hard on Nick Carter. Go Backstreet Boys.

While Noah took his afternoon nap, they sang each other "Happy Birthday." The third time around catching up on missed birthdays, they weren't nearly as emotional as the first two. After stuffing her face on white layer cake with strawberry cream filling and pink frosting—because morning sickness hadn't kicked in—Eva decided to share her news. Daisy had come out of hiding in time to lick leftover icing from their plates, and Lacy mindlessly pet her calico cat as she feasted.

"I'm pregnant," Eva said, just throwing it out there.

"What?" Lacy appeared to have just seen a UFO.

Eva nodded, her eyes filling up, then Lacy dived for her and they hugged tight. "And you're...happy? Sad?"

"Mixed up." Her sister's face went blurry. "Part of me is amazed how easy it turned out for me to get pregnant. We figure it happened the night in the limousine."

"Wait. What?" There went another UFO.

Oh, right, Eva had kept their little romp on their first meeting to herself. "Uh, yeah," she said with a coy smile. "We went a little crazy the night we met."

"I can't believe it."

Eva sighed, her shoulders lifting and dropping with the breath. "It's true."

Lacy's head shook, still in disbelief. "You never let on. All this time, I thought it was a slow build, that we were fixing you up, and that Zack and I were secretly manipulating your future."

Finally, after days of brooding, Eva laughed. "You really are pushy, but seriously, you don't think you're that powerful, do you?"

"Twin power, sister." Their laugh turned ironic and died quickly as they got back to the point. "What does Joe think? I couldn't help but notice he hasn't been around the last couple of days." Her brows bunched with worry.

"He's a busy man. The last thing he needs is another scandal. Even though the other ones are made up."

"Is that what he said?"

Eva shook her head. "Nope. That's what I said, and that's how I want it."

"But that still didn't answer my question."

No, it didn't, because he'd behaved like a prince and she was the holdout. Her heart still pinched remembering the moment. "He says we should go for it."

Lacy clapped in relief. "That's wonderful!"

"No. It isn't. I've always secretly dreamed of a romantic proposal from a guy who loved me for me, not because I was carrying his baby."

Now Lacy looked concerned. "But Joe is honest. If he chooses to do the honorable thing, it's because he really cares about you."

Eva had heard him call her *mi amor* the night she'd taken the test and he'd done the sweetest thing of putting her to bed, then curling up with her for support and comfort. She'd never felt more protected in her life, and she didn't doubt his sincerity. But still…

"It's too early for me to deal with everything. Do you mind if we change the subject?"

Lacy came beside Eva and put her arm around her shoulders. "Whatever you want. I'm here for you."

"Then tell me more about Dad."

For the next few minutes, Lacy went on and on about their redheaded father, John, and how wonderful he was, aware how much Eva needed to take her mind off her current worries. Then something occurred to Eva, probably because she was pregnant, but also because she'd missed ever meeting her natural father.

"I know we told my mom we'd leave things as they are with the closed surrogacy. But our birth mother is probably in her fifties and still alive somewhere out there. Now that I'm pregnant, I'd really like to know her medical history. Of course, I'd really like to meet her, too, but maybe we could use this as an opportunity."

"You want to ask Joe to help us find her?"

"I do. She sacrificed nine months of her life in her twenties, when most young women are traveling or going to college or starting their own families. She did that so our parents could have children."

"She got paid well for it, too."

"True, but it's still a sacrifice. Can you imagine carrying twins? Plus, she gave us our shared middle name. She made our existence possible, carried us, then had the courage to give us up." Eva's hand rested on her stomach. "I think she's worth meeting, don't you?"

Lacy nodded in solidarity.

"And if there's anything in her health history I should know, now is the time to find out."

"The election is a week from Tuesday. Once that's over, I'm sure Joe will be glad to take what we know and track her down for us. There's got to be a legal way to go about it."

"Yes," Eva said, remembering. "He was more than willing the night we called my mom, but we shut him down."

"You don't mind dealing with him in that capacity?"

"Lacy, I don't want Joe out of my life, not when he's just walked in. I have feelings for him. I'm just disappointed things got rushed because we couldn't keep our hands off each other."

Lacy gave a sad-sack laugh. "I know the feeling. I'm helpless around Zack."

"Yeah, but you guys are engaged. If something happened now, you'd know for sure he loved you first."

Lacy took Eva's hand and petted it, as if she was Daisy. "For weeks now, I've seen the way he looks at you and acts around you. Trust me, you're not forcing him into something he doesn't already want to do."

Monday afternoon, at his law office, Joe dealt with as much of the finishing touches to his campaign as possible when his mind was completely on Eva and the pregnancy. She'd insisted she needed time to think through the situation, and because he loved her—he'd definitely figured that out now—he gave it to her.

The price was high, though. Each moment away, doubt entered his thoughts. Not on his end, but about her wanting him.

"Aha!" Mike said, from across the room. For the last hour, he'd been scrolling though the daily emails, reading and replying with Joe's input. "I had one of the high school volunteers snoop around on the internet and guess what we found out."

Always appreciative of his lifelong friend's help on his campaigns, Joe patiently watched and waited for Mike to give the full dramatic affect.

"That Kitty Mittens is indeed Louella Barnstable." Mike rose, hand raised, finger pointing toward the ceiling, like a lawyer deliberating a big case during closing statements. "Evidently she's used some senior citizen friends with a lot of free time on their hands to drive around and look for you in compromising situations."

Joe pulled in his chin. "Seriously? How bored must someone be?" He sighed. *Wait till they find out Eva's pregnant, they'll have a field day.*

"Perfect timing," Mike said. "You can drop a bombshell on her tonight at the interview."

"Nope. Nope. Not taking that route. It will make me as bad as her."

"But she deserves a public shaming."

Joe laughed. "What century are you from?"

"The barrio, brother. You don't want to prove what a lousy person and therefore mayor she'd be with this new information? Get real."

Joe shook his head. "All her shenanigans haven't changed the polls. Didn't you just tell me I'm still ahead?"

"Yes, but…"

"Let's just let this election play itself out in a natural way, then you can divulge her dirty little secret after I'm mayor. Though I'd rather you just let it lie."

Joe went back to focusing on preparing for that night. There was one thing he wanted to use the interview for, and it was on a personal level. He'd had an old sick feeling souring his gut since Eva found out she was pregnant. Not because she was pregnant, no, that part was fine with him. Great, even. He'd gone out on the limb and said he wanted to go for it with her. To be a couple and have their kid together. Deep inside, he knew he wanted to marry her, too, but worried she'd freak out if he asked her.

Why? Because he wasn't good enough for her.

Same old song, second verse.

Well, he was sick of carrying that worn-out feeling around with him and needed to prove Eva wasn't Victoria. Not by a long shot.

He remembered what his mother used to say after that breakup: *What girl wouldn't want you?* He had a lot to offer, damn right. So why wasn't Eva jumping at the chance?

He was thrilled about their baby, but she needed to come around on that end on her own. Well, there was something he could prove, and doing it publicly was a risk.

No risk, no gain. That saying he'd learned himself, and was why he'd chosen Stanford Law School.

Eva wanted a romantic proposal; well, hopefully, his publicly admitting how he felt about her on local TV would be romantic enough.

Aching for Joe every day, settling for mere phone calls, Eva went on with life, waiting out the election before dealing with their personal P-bomb. Noah was a huge help. She loved him with everything she had. She'd brought him home at a mere two weeks and stumbled her way through being a new mom. At least she knew how to care for a baby now. She glanced at her son, napping in bliss, and smiled, her heart swelling with love.

The early signs of pregnancy were setting in. Tender breasts, queasiness. Work could only distract her for so long. Truth was, she missed Joe with everything she had.

Someone knocked on the door, and worried it might wake Noah, she rushed to open it. As if hearing her silent wish, there he was. "Joe." She caught her breath.

He pushed through to where she stood and took

her in his arms. "Hello, gorgeous." He kissed her hair. "I couldn't stay away another second."

Being held by him proved how much she'd longed for him. She grinned with joy as she buried her face in his neck, savoring his scent and the feel of his soft skin. "I've missed you, too."

"How are you feeling?" He pulled back, glancing at her and then toward the region of her abdomen.

"Feeling the changes." Of course, he knew all this with his daily calls. They'd kept each other up-to-date while managing to avoid saying the most important things. Being in person, seeing him after several days, was all she'd longed for.

His eyes brightened. "You are?"

"Yeah. Sick to my stomach half the day, exhausted the rest."

He grimaced. "Sorry."

"Nah, it's not so bad." She could be honest with Joe. "Maybe kind of sucky but also kind of amazing."

They hugged and kissed again, and she sensed he didn't want to let her go. That part was wonderful, feeling wanted. Loved?

"I'm here to insist you come with me tonight to Little River Valley Closed Circuit TV. I've got an interview scheduled and you can't miss it."

She drew back her head, grateful he'd yanked her out of her thought. "You sure?"

"Absolutely."

"What about the gossip mill?"

"Mike found out who the real Kitty Mittens is."

"Seriously?"

He told her the whole story as she took him to Lacy's kitchen and made him some coffee. This was how it was supposed to be, the two of them against the world. Friends. Lovers, and sooner than expected, or dreamed, parents. She handed him the mug after hearing him out. Wow, that Louella Barnstable played dirty. And when Joe had the opportunity to use his elbows, he took the high road. That was why she loved him. There was that word again.

"Then, of course, I'll come."

That night at the interview, Eva was as nervous as though she was the one having to do live TV. Her palms were clammy and, maybe it was the bright lights, the back of her neck was damp under her hair as she watched Joe get tested for sound and have a few shiny spots on his face blotted out with powder. She admired how he did whatever was necessary for what he considered a privilege, to continue to do a tough job, being mayor. It took a special type of person to want that responsibility. That said so much for Joe. Where others ran from responsibility, he walked toward it. Like now, with the pregnancy.

Mike was in attendance, and the middle-aged male interviewer, then her. Other than the small TV crew, they were the only ones in the studio. And she was honored to be Joe's one guest. The sweet thing was, no one needed to know she was there, either. It was between her and Joe. She blew a mental raspberry. *Take that, Kitty Mittens.*

The local newscaster began the interview with the usual questions about Joe's history. Joe was candid as he told a brief story about his impoverished background, how being a first-generation American had shaped him. He'd shared how his parents believed in the American dream and had worked all their lives to achieve it. Joe was honored to be the first in his family to attend college, thanks to the sacrifices his parents had made.

The interviewer seemed to be enthralled, then skillfully brought the subject around to the current election and his opponent. Diplomatically, Joe found a way to compliment his challenger for being eager to help their city by running for the job, but he stopped short of mentioning any scandals she'd hinted at. Except one.

"I know my challenger has concerns about my student loans, which I am paying off little by little. But even that is part of the American dream these days, right? I've read there are almost forty-eight million Americans in debt from student loans." He looked at the camera. "Louella, it's a thing."

The interviewer laughed at his little joke. Eva admired how he'd managed to name her and call her out without coming off as mean.

"Your campaign slogan says, Locally Grown,

Promising to Keep Little River Valley Sustainable.
Why don't you tell us how you plan to do that?"

Joe went on to cover his plans for running the city.
Much of what he said was a repeat from his campaign
rallies and the debate, but Mike reminded Eva how
a candidate had to pound home their points to get
people to remember. He hoped people who hadn't
seen or heard him before might tune in to the TV.

After ten minutes, the interviewer gave Joe free
rein. "Tell us something we don't know about your
candidacy."

Joe used one finger to scratch the side of his
mouth as he thought, for the first time seeming un-
sure, nervous, even, about being in the spotlight.
Then something changed in his expression.

"I fell in love on a lot of different levels on the
campaign trail. First and foremost, thanks to a little
lady named Savannah Schuster. You may have heard
of her and the Dreams Come True wish?"

The interviewer filled in the television audience
about the request and the dinner that followed, as
a recap.

"And we've become great friends." Touched by his
retelling, Eva smiled, deep in memory. "A guy never
expects to fall in love on the campaign trail, but then
I met Eva." Hearing her name, she snapped back
into the conversation. "How ironic that we met on a
Dreams Come True date. True I was with the other
woman, Savannah, and Eva was the chaperone."

Though fewer than ten people were in the room, his remark got a good laugh. Then Joe went sincere, his eyes soft and serene, the interviewer obviously empathetic to the turn of the interview. Because it was good stuff for ratings.

"Because of Savannah, I met a little boy named Noah, too, and I'm crazy about him. I'm crazy about his mother, too. Did I mention that already?" Another laugh from the interviewer. "And I'm sure you've heard some rumors about that part. They're about the person who set up my date with Savannah, and if it hadn't been for that dinner, where Savannah and I were accompanied by a chaperone, I never would have met Eva."

The interviewer sat back and let Joe naturally riff about what happened during campaigning.

"Looking back, I knew right from the start she was special, and, well, inconvenient or not, I went for it—letting myself fall for her. Because how often does a gift like that fall in a guy's lap? Especially while he's campaigning? All I can hope is she feels the same, because I'm hoping she'll become my wife."

Joe seemed to pull out of his confession in time to say one last thing. "And if that isn't putting myself on the line, I don't know what is."

Nearly gasping, Eva searched for a chair and sat with the help of Mike, who looked as shocked as she felt.

"I wanted to beat the gossip mill with this scoop."

He didn't name a name, but it was quite evident to anyone following the election whom Joe meant. "So if I'm fortunate enough to get reelected, my first order of business will be to get engaged and married."

The interviewer couldn't have looked happier about the scoop, and Eva couldn't have been more mixed up.

Though the next part of the interview was a blur to her, Joe ended by thanking the station for inviting him and asking the people to vote their conscience. Then, during his brief recap on why he hoped to be mayor again and how he loved Little River Valley, Eva found the strength to get up and run outside the studio.

She didn't want any extra ears around when she said what she had to say to Joe.

As she knew he would, at his first chance, Joe followed and found her in the small patio area outside the studio. She turned and watched him approach wearing a concerned yet baffled expression.

Insisting on not giving him the first word, she blurted her gut reaction. "You used me." Her old and familiar fear did the talking, thanks to Lawrence taking those bets at her expense. "For ratings. How dare you!"

His visage sharpened; he'd clearly taken offense. "That's not the way I see it, but I'm beginning to think maybe I'll never be good enough for you."

Chapter Thirteen

Eva and Joe were six feet apart, staring at each other in a standoff. Eva made clear the old baggage they'd promised to trash some time back was still alive and running the show. So did Joe.

"You didn't ask me if it was okay to share our personal business. I'm surprised you didn't leak the pregnancy!"

"I would never do that." She'd stung him with the remark, and his words may have come out sharper than normal, but between the two of them, only he could claim to be close to calm.

"But it's okay to tell all Little River Valley we're involved, when I only just told my twin sister last week?"

"That wasn't how I saw it." Again, his words were measured and steady as though dealing with someone ready to explode. Which she was. He had a knack for de-escalating situations, and right now it annoyed the hell out of her.

"It didn't occur to you that you were using me? To get good ratings and votes!" Furious, she waited for him to say something, but he held back, seeming baffled by her accusations. Would she have to spell it out? "I've been here before, Joe, feeling humiliated in public, having no control over personal information, and I swore then to never let that happen again."

Joe took a step closer, anger pooling in his just-can't-win gaze. "I was trying to be romantic." He ground the words through a clenched jaw, clearly at the end of his patience. "You told me that was how you wanted a proposal to be. Obviously, I fell flat. Again. Not my intention. But from my end, I just told anyone watching that interview how I feel about you." He pointed toward the studio before relaxing his arms and lifting his palms. "That's not *using* you for personal gain, that's admitting the truth. I love you. Why isn't that good enough?"

While feeling a bit like Goldilocks with first too cold, now too hot, waiting for just right, a bolt of wisdom hit her between the eyes. Their old insecurities were still running roughshod over them. This conversation could put an end to them if they continued on this path. Eva took a sharp breath, attempting to clear her head, but failed.

She sucked a deep breath. "I need more time," was all she could manage to say before walking away.

The next twenty-four hours were a blur. All Eva wanted to do was sleep. Her morning sickness lasted all day, as she was convinced most of it was being sick over the state of her relationship with Joe.

What relationship? She'd pretty much insured he'd give up on getting more involved with a crazy woman like her.

She clung to her pillow like it was her last remaining friend.

Lacy had the good sense to stay out of her way, while still sticking close by, and taking on the lion's share of Noah's care.

When too much sleep gave her a headache, she thought. Flat on her back, eyes trained on the ceiling, she forced herself to go over the latest turn of events.

Fact: Joe had fearlessly said out loud that he loved her. A guy feeling forced into marriage would never do that.

Fact: As she'd once been used and humiliated by a man she'd trusted, Joe had also been abused by a woman he could never be "good enough" for.

With her running away, leaving him standing alone at the TV studio, she'd humiliated him, the man who'd just told the entire city of Little River Valley he loved her.

How must he feel?

Fact: The last person on the planet Joe had acted like was Lawrence.

And the last person on earth she wanted to be like was Victoria. Yet that was exactly how she'd acted.

Another bout of queasiness had her bolting for the bathroom.

An hour later, after she'd showered and dressed, she quietly entered the kitchen where Lacy fed Noah lunch.

"Hey" was all Lacy said, obviously trying to be low key and stay out of Eva's mess.

"Hi," Eva whispered while hearing a lawn mower in the distance. When Noah saw his mom and fussed for her, she picked him up and squeezed with all her heart. "My sweet boy." He gurgled and kicked his legs.

"Da," he said, his sound for many things, one of which was "down."

"He's been okay," Lacy said, standing back, letting Eva hold her son.

"Thank you."

"Not necessary. Let me get you something to eat or drink?"

"Don't really want anything." She let Noah down.

"But you need to eat."

She sat at the kitchen table and stared out the window. The mower had gone quiet in time for a leaf blower to start up. She squinted her eyes tight and rubbed her temples.

"You're probably dehydrated and have low blood sugar. At least have some toast and green tea."

Eva inhaled and nodded. Lacy was right, and she was on it, already putting bread in the toaster and heating water for the tea.

"I've been doing a lot of thinking, as you can imagine."

"I don't even know what happened, but you don't have to say anything until you're ready."

In that moment, Eva loved her sister like she never had before. Lacy was being exactly what she needed in that moment, a little motherly, a lot of friend, and a whole bunch of understanding.

As she sipped the tea and nibbled the dry toast, she let Lacy in on what had happened and all she'd been thinking about since.

After giving a long, tender hug, Lacy straightened to a stand and cleared her throat. "You know Joe's out front mowing the heck out of his lawn."

Eva slowly inhaled, willing herself to stay calm and be strong, to do what needed to be done for her sake, for Joe's, and for their future. "Out front, you said?"

Lacy smiled encouragingly and nodded.

Eva went to Joe, who was shirtless, which wasn't playing fair. He stopped pushing the mower and turned it off, then wiped his brow with his bare forearm, watching and waiting for Eva to make the next move. She stepped up to him and put a slightly trembling hand on his cheek, and, thankfully, he let her, without flinching, especially after the way she'd just treated him yesterday.

"I'm sorry," she said. "I've been doing nothing but thinking and, well, you're right. What you did was a beautiful thing. I took it all wrong." She kissed him gently. "But you took my response the wrong way, too." Lifting her second hand, she held his moist face, staring into his mahogany-tinted eyes. "My reaction wasn't about you not being good enough for me. It was me still being tangled up in my old hurt. You're doing the same thing with yours. Please, let's stop. For the sake of us."

She could tell she'd gotten through to him. He reached for her and pulled her close, both holding tight with the knowledge they might have lost each other if she hadn't wised up and he'd continued to let her walk away.

After a long, thorough kiss, Joe looked into Eva's eyes. "We may not have started up in the right order, but I wouldn't change a thing, because I love you."

He'd publicly worn his love on his sleeve in yesterday's interview; it was time for her to say her truth. "I love you, too."

Opportunity seemed to twinkle in his eyes. "Then you'll marry me, right?"

A tiny, relieved laugh crossed her lips. She'd be a fool not to, but the guy needed serious schooling on romantic proposals.

Less than week later, election night had rushed up before Eva and Joe were ready. They'd hardly had a chance to be together since the TV interview, what with his final sprint toward reelection and her morning—let's face it, all-day—sickness, Dreams Come True obligations and caring for Noah. Now Eva, Lacy, Savannah and Zack pushed through the doors of the campaign headquarters at Olive, where the victory party would be held. Emma's lifelong babysitter from next door, Mrs. Worthington, watched Noah and Emma back at Zack's house. Everyone seemed bent on ignoring the other possibility—a concession speech. They didn't need a huge space, being a small city, but Olive had moved all the furniture to the sides of the room, leaving the bar-height tables along the walls for later, when drinks would get served. For now, they were good for leaning on. Earlier, Zack, under the instruction of Mike, had built a small stage from which Joe could give his acceptance speech. Assuming he would win. She didn't want to put a hex on it, but really!

If Eva believed the latest polls, Joe and Louella were neck and neck, but something about those statistics didn't ring true. How could anyone not love Joe?

The silly question made her laugh to herself. She'd

done her best not to and look how that had turned out. She was head over heels for a guy in a profession she abhorred. Yeah, one of life's little har-har lessons.

She imagined Joe's bright, handsome face, then Louella's sourpuss expressions. Mayor Kitty Mittens? Never!

One day she might think about what she'd learned since meeting Joe, but right now, she was tense and biting cuticles over the early returns. So were Lacy and Savannah. Her girl crew. The good news was, unlike national elections, there were only a few thousand votes to count in Little River Valley. If all went as planned, they'd know the results by 9:00 p.m.

She'd worn a dress for the occasion, something she'd bought at the one and only department store in town. The Little River Valley Mercantile Co-op, a large, one-story shop carrying a diverse assortment of items from household and kitchen items, to shoes and men's and women's clothing. They had a surprising line of chic, yet casual wear to choose from. She'd found a flattering white-and-blue-patterned dress with a V-neck, three-quarter sleeves and shaping seams at the waist to hide the tiny change in her waist since becoming pregnant. The overlapping large and small navy blue stripes created an optical illusion as the fitting skirt playfully fell to her knees. She'd accessorized the look with red earrings, preferring understatement than overkill, still feeling surprisingly patriotic. She'd done it solely for Joe, would he notice?

It was seven, and Joe, accompanied by Mike, made an early appearance. The crowd of fifty or so applauded, and Savannah cupped hands around her mouth to give what sounded more like a hog call than a cheer. Joe grinned and waved with both hands at everyone, wearing a casual dark suit with a pale blue shirt unbuttoned at the collar, no tie in sight. Looking sexy. As always he made her heart flutter, especially when his dark eyes found hers. After an obligatory hand-shaking session around the room, he made his way to Eva, Lacy and Savannah.

Not caring who saw, he kissed her, pulling her close and hugging like a man both excited and nervous.

"No matter what happens, you're the winner in my book," she whispered over his ear, giving him her full support.

Her words had a surprising effect on him as he stopped, blinked and humbly glanced at the floor before coming back to her loving gaze. "Thank you" was all he said. Then after another thought, "You look great. Like a politician's sexy wife."

She scoffed. Lacy laughed hard. Savannah apparently didn't hear a thing, most likely due to all the background noise.

Eva hoped he understood her meaning that no matter what happened, he was and always would be good enough for her. From his heartfelt response, she suspected he did.

"If you don't mind, I've got to…" he said, hesitating to finish his thought.

"Work the room, I know. Hey, why not take Savannah with you, she'd love it!"

"Great idea." Joe held out his elbow for Savannah to take hold, then proceeded to escort her around the room to the various townspeople, including city council members and school board staff. She wondered who attended Louella's party. Probably a lot of outside business folks chomping at the chance to get a hold of Little River Valley for property development.

Please win, Joe, please, please, please. True, she didn't live there, but since having temporarily moved in with Lacy, she had a strong sense of community with the place. It was impossible to stay uninvolved here, unlike in Santa Barbara, where she lived behind a large gate. Little River Valley was just fine as it was, no need to upgrade or expand a thing. The perfectly good dress she wore was evidence they didn't need big department chains. Or any other chains in town.

An hour and a half later, after two rounds of delicious appetizers and wine donated by Olive—Eva skipped the wine, instead sipping sparkling water—Mike hopped up on the stage. Before he could speak, Eva's gaze, along with Joe's, drifted to the entrance, where two more visitors had arrived. Joe rushed to the older Hispanic couple and hugged them tight. His parents! They'd made it, and Joe couldn't have looked happier. He started toward Eva with one parent under each arm. Before he got to her, Mike tapped the microphone for a sound check, causing severe feedback. Savannah grabbed her ears and made a face. Eva wondered if such loud noises bothered tiny fetuses, as her hand flew to her tummy. She quickly introduced herself and shook hands with an older version of handsome Joe and a small woman with determined eyes and midnight black hair with silver bands at the temples. His parents, the people who made him the wonderful man she'd come to love.

"We just got word," Mike said, "that the last votes have been counted and the tally is in." The room went quiet in anticipation. Mike gave his unique toothy grin as he looked around with pride. "Drumroll, please," he said, causing Zack and several other people to tap the tabletops in syncopation. Mike laughed and motioned for Joe to step up on the stage. Leaving his obviously proud parents with a drink in their hands, he joined his best friend in the front of the room. Mike lifted his right arm and then brought it down to grasp Joe's hand in an exaggerated but solid handshake.

Eva's pulse intensified.

"I'd like to introduce our mayor, reelected in a *landslide,* Joe Aguirre!"

Applause thundered through the room, hoots and howls, and Eva made it a point to watch Joe's parents join in the celebration, their faces bright with pride as they listened attentively to their son's victory speech.

By the time Joe had finished, he'd thanked just about everyone in the room, beginning with his parents and Mike, and including Zack and Lacy and Savannah.

"Now I'd like to introduce someone who wasn't around for the first term but will hopefully become an integral part of my second. You may know her as Savannah Schuster's escort, but I call her the woman I love. Eva?"

With her face burning, and applause swelling, she didn't hesitate to make her way to the stage. She took Joe's outstretched hand to help take the three small makeshift steps, then let him pull her tight to his side after a quick kiss. Without thinking she waved at everyone, as though she'd been the one running for office. It made her laugh and feel a little silly. She hadn't thought about this aspect, had never wanted anything to do with such things, yet, like all the others in this room, she was swept up under Joe's spell. Happy and proud to be taking part.

After several torturous minutes in the spotlight, where thankfully Joe did all the talking, Mike led the toasts, and things finally died down. They stepped off the stage. She looked for his parents, but they were already gone. The crowd mingled among itself, and Joe had Eva at his side. He walked her to a dark and quiet corner.

"You know the other day when we kind of sort of got engaged?" he said, leaning one hand against the wall.

"We did?" She pressed her shoulder against the same wall.

"Yeah, I was mowing the lawn and said we should go for it and you agreed."

"Ah, yes, that. I recall something along those lines, sure."

"Well, I'd like to add a disclaimer."

She rolled, putting her back against the wall, and folded her arms. "Now you're talking like a lawyer, and a politician. That's not fair. And definitely not romantic."

"Hear me out. That's the part I'm working on. I, Joe Aguirre…"

"Mayor Joe Aguirre," she teasingly corrected.

"Yes. Oh, wait." He dropped to a knee and took her hand as she stiffened.

"I, Mayor Joe Aguirre, ask your hand in marriage—"

She'd been walking around spouting that finding her sister after thirty-one years was the greatest thing to happen in her life since adopting Noah. But this, being pregnant and in love, had now become by far the biggest surprise of her life.

Never surer of anything, she jumped right in. "I'd love to marry you."

He raised a finger indicating there was more. "—on

the condition you'll live here with me in Little River Valley in my humble home."

"Just like the constituents you represent." It made total sense.

"Yes. In the house two doors down from your sister."

"Who'll be marrying and moving in with Zack."

"True, but not right away?"

"No date's set."

"Wait a second," he said, drawing her back to the fact he was still on one knee. "We're getting off track." He took her other hand. "Will you marry me?"

"Under all those conditions?"

He sighed. "Yes, including me loving and being Noah's dad as well as our bambino's."

He spoke straight from his heart. Overcome, she gripped his hands, her throat tight with emotions and words she wanted to share with him but couldn't. Her eyes filled with tears of joy as she joined him, kneeling.

"Yes. Of course, I'll marry you," she said looking into the eyes of the man she couldn't wait to share the rest of her life with. Joe.

Chapter Fourteen

The reveal

"Okay, on the count of three let's both step out," Lacy said from the adjacent dressing room in the bridal shop in Santa Barbara.

"Are you ready?" Eva gave up on the top half of the zipper, positive her arms couldn't contort to that extent.

"Just about." Lacy said, then quickly followed with "Shoot."

"We need some help over here," Eva spoke up. The wedding dress attendant, who'd been so helpful all afternoon as they'd tried on dress after dress off the rack, rushed to help. Lacy had insisted this was the way she always bought her clothes, and that was how she intended to find her wedding dress. Happy to share a double wedding with her twin, Eva went along.

"We both need help with our zippers and last button." As the attendant finished Eva's dress first, Eva called out to Lacy across the way. "I think I've found mine, how about you?"

"I'm positive this is the dress I want to get married in."

Once Lacy found out Joe had asked Eva to marry him, she'd run it by Zack first, then insisted they have a double wedding. They'd finished their grouped birthday celebrations and it only made sense to share this most special day. They'd even insisted they'd walk each other down the aisle, since their father couldn't.

"I can't wait to see yours!" Eva said, smoothing her hands down the front of her dress.

"Same here with yours!"

"There you go, ma'am," the attendant said, making Eva feel ancient even though she understood the older woman originally from Europe was just being respectful. "Now I go help your sister."

"Thank you." Eva turned side to side, admiring the chic outfit. It was the most perfect wedding dress she could ever imagine. The romantic, fairy-tale dress with jeweled off-the-shoulder straps and

V-neck slit, fitted bodice and flared skirt was every-thing she'd ever dreamed of.

"Oh," the attendant said taking in a quick breath after entering Lacy's stall.

Eva's heart sank with the worry that her sister had chosen something that didn't agree with the fine taste of the establishment Eva had dragged her to. Lacy had protested the whole way, saying *I always buy off the rack, and why should I change my habits now?* With great patience Eva had explained that in essence they *would* be buying off the rack, just with the option of having the dresses altered to perfection.

They'd each grabbed dress after dress and tried on one after the other for three hours now. Then, after one last pass through their size section, losing track of who took what, and deciding not to look at each other's dresses until they'd tried them on, they'd made their last trip to the changing room.

"Everything all right?" Eva called out, com-pletely in love with her dress, worrying Lacy would never want to try a fancy place like this again if she couldn't find the dress of her dreams.

"Perfect," Lacy said. "It's perfect. This is the one."

"Oh, dear," the attendant said quietly.

Eva hoped for the best, but her gut tightened over what she might find Lacy wearing. "Okay, on the count of three!"

Lacy started the count. "One…"

"Two," Eva joined.

"Three!" they said together as Eva pushed open her dressing room door and stepped into the main parlor. Lacy had done the same, and Eva eagerly looked at her sister. She sucked a breath, thinking she was looking into one of the long panel of mirrors. How in the name of a hundred dresses could they choose the exact same one?

Lacy started laughing. "We chose the same one!"

"We never dress alike. How did this happen?" The irony quickly turned to giggles as the sisters stepped together and stood side by side in front of the main mirror, looking more like twins than they ever had before. Which was a big deal because they looked uncannily identical under normal circumstances. With them wearing wedding dresses, the exact wedding dresses, the effect was shocking. Especially since Eva had made up for the five-pound difference between them by the middle of the first trimester.

"Is *thees* a *problème*?" the attendant asked tentatively.

Lacy made her usual happy-go-lucky face. "Not for me. Eva?" she looked expectantly at Eva, waiting.

Taking a second to formulate her thoughts, Eva studied Lacy, knowing all she had to do was hesitate or suggest maybe they should be a bit more individual on the biggest day of their lives. The biggest day since they'd found each other. If she did, Lacy would lay down that dress. For her. She'd walk away from the most perfect dress in the world for her, just so

Eva could have it all to herself. Well, no way was that going to happen.

"I think this is the best idea ever!"

One month later, the wedding day

Eva and Lacy put the finishing touches on their makeup and carefully placed the wedding veils on their heads, each helping the other. The veils turned out to be the one thing to set them apart. Eva's was short and stylish, and Lacy's longer, more traditional. They took one last look at each other and hugged carefully.

"I can't think of a better way to share my wedding than with you," Eva said. "And our husbands, of course," she quickly added the most important part, the men they loved.

"I know exactly what you mean," Lacy said, now holding hands with Eva. "Finding each other, picking up where we never had the chance to start, has meant more than anything to me."

With Joe's help, they'd moved forward on locating their birth mother. The name Desirae turned out to belong to the delivery nurse the day they'd been born. She was still alive but refused to divulge the identity of their mother. However, following up on the name Taylor in the birth records for the day twins were born in the small Santa Paula hospital, Joe said he had a lead. An address. Of course, it was outdated, but who knew where it might lead?

"I just wish…" Lacy continued.

"We can go on forever wishing we'd been together all our lives," Eva cautioned. "It didn't happen and thinking that way will keep us sad. We need to let that go. This is supposed to be the most joyous day of our lives, so let's take every second and breathe it in."

"I know. You're right." Lacy squeezed her hands.

Eva swore she saw that mischievous gaze that often crept into her sister's eyes. "What?" She lifted her sister's veil to get a better look.

"You said not to dwell on it, but you know we never got to dress like each other and play tricks on people, and, well, I just had a wicked idea."

Eva pulled in her chin, easily reading her twin's thoughts, and considering a most cruel trick that had no place at a wedding ceremony. And yet… "That would mean I walk down the aisle on the left."

"Absolutely. And me on the right. The perfect test."

"What's your bet? Before or after the veil lift? Wait, no bets." Eva would never bet money on Joe with a dare.

"Let's see what plays out."

"It's risky, but why not? We only live once."

"It's a great test, don't you think?"

Guilt tiptoed in. "Do we need to test them?"

"No. But it would certainly make our wedding one to never be forgotten."

"I'm pretty sure it's going to be that anyway."

"Still…"

Eva lifted her veil, not wanting to mess it up while they snickered about their devilish plans.

As the small church wedding planner reentered the room, they quickly covered their faces with their veils and stopped laughing.

"It's time, ladies," the planner said. "Lacy, you're on the left. Eva, the right."

"Got it," Eva said, stepping into the left. Their little naughty plan was really going to happen.

A few short minutes later, with church music swirling through the air and tingles covering every part of Eva's body, she made it a point not to look at her sister again. Otherwise she might cry her eyes out. Together, they began the wedding march as Emma led the way as both flower girl and ring bearer. Noah was still too young to be trusted.

The entrance song—from *The Princess Bride*—had been another unanimous choice for the sisters. The guys were quick to approve it, since the walk down the aisle belonged to their future wives, them and them alone.

Eva tried her best to keep it all together, knowing Lacy did the same. Assuring each other as they did by holding hands for support. They wore the same dresses and looked exactly alike, the only thing setting them apart being their respective veils. Eva's was a birdcage veil that swept across her face to her chin in a fashionable style. Lacy's was a more classic two-tier midlength that fell to her waist in the back and to her shoulder in front.

Zack and Joe had never seen their dresses, as was the custom, or the veils.

As they approached the altar, Eva's eyes drifted to Joe standing tall, looking so incredibly handsome in his tux, his dark hair combed to perfection. His eyes fixed on... Lacy. It felt all wrong, made her want to drift into her sister's lane, but they'd made a devious plan and would carry it out until it counted. Taking their vows.

Before Joe could notice, she shifted her gaze to Zack. Dark blond hair tamed with product, a dashing smile, sparkling green eyes. Gorgeous, but not the man she loved, though Lacy was a lucky woman, too.

They reached the spot where they were supposed to wait for their grooms to take their hand and bring them to the pastor. Deep in thought about what a mistake they'd made on their wedding day, Eva stared straight ahead, worrying about the outcome. Whose idea had it been? Lacy's!

Since Eva had switched with Lacy, playing out what now seemed like a horrible idea on such an important day, her hands trembled. She'd lost all the bold-faced courage she and Lacy had come up with to play such a rotten trick on their men. What had gotten into them?

Years of being separated, missing out on things like pretending to be each other, that was what. Still… Today? Of all days?

She waited and looked at Zack again, who tossed a quick glance toward Joe, who happened to be searching for Zack's eyes. Weren't they supposed to be making googly eyes at their brides, not each other?

Eva's fingers quavered, making it hard to hold her bouquet still. The men nodded to each other and stepped forward. Zack crossed in front of Eva, heading toward Lacy. With a little fancy footwork himself, Joe stepped into his place in front of Eva.

Even veiled, they hadn't fooled them for one second. Apparently, it would take more than the same dress to trick the man she loved.

Joe gave a knowing wink and held out his elbow. "Nice try," he said under his breath.

With a demure grin and full blush, feeling beyond foolish, she took his arm as he led her to their spot at the altar. Standing in front of the pastor, ready and waiting to take her vows, Eva knew without a doubt that Joe was the one and only man in the entire world meant to be her husband.

And no identical-twin elementary school prank could prove otherwise.

* * * * *

*Don't miss the surprising finale of
the Taylor Triplets miniseries,*

The Reluctant Fiancée

*available May 2020 from
Harlequin Special Edition!
And find Lacy's story,*

Cooking Up Romance

*available now wherever Harlequin books
and ebooks are sold!*

COMING NEXT MONTH FROM

HARLEQUIN
SPECIAL EDITION

Available April 21, 2020

#2761 BETTING ON A FORTUNE
The Fortunes of Texas: Rambling Rose • by Nancy Robards Thompson
Ashley Fortune is furious Rodrigo Mendoza has been hired to consult on her new restaurant and vows to send him packing. Soon her resentment turns to attraction, but Rodrigo won't mix business with pleasure. When her sister gives her a self-help book that promises to win him over in a week, Ashley goes all in to land Rodrigo's heart!

#2762 THEIR SECRET SUMMER FAMILY
The Bravos of Valentine Bay • by Christine Rimmer
Officer Dante Santangelo doesn't "do" relationships, but the busy single dad happily agrees to a secret summer fling with younger, free-spirited Gracie Bravo. It's the perfect arrangement. Until Gracie falls for Dante, his adorable twins and their ever-present fur baby!

#2763 HER SECOND FOREVER
The Brands of Montana • by Joanna Sims
The car accident that left her permanently injured made Lee Macbeth only more determined to help others with disabilities. Now there's a charming cowboy doing a stint of community service at her therapeutic riding facility and he wants more than the self-sufficient widow. Despite their powerful mutual attraction, Lee won't risk falling for Mr. Totally Wrong...will she?

#2764 STARTING OVER IN WICKHAM FALLS
Wickham Falls Weddings • by Rochelle Alers
Georgina Powell is finally moving out of her parents' house after years of carrying her mother's grief. At thirty-two years old, she's ready for a fresh start. She just didn't expect it to come in the form of Langston Cooper, the famed war correspondent who recently returned to buy Wickham Falls's local paper. But as she opens her own business, his role as editor in chief may steer him in a different direction—away from their future together.

#2765 THE RELUCTANT FIANCÉE
The Taylor Triplets • by Lynne Marshall
When Brynne Taylor breaks off her engagement to Paul Capriati, she knows her life is going to change. But when two women who claim to be triplets to her children show up in her small Utah town, it's a lot more change than she ever expected. Now she's digging up long-buried family secrets and navigating her relationship with her ex-fiancé. Does she actually want to get married?

#2766 THE NANNY'S FAMILY WISH
The Culhanes of Cedar River • by Helen Lacey
Annie Jamison has dreamed of capturing the heart of David Culhane McCall. But she knows the workaholic widower sees her only as a caregiver to his children. Until her resignation lands on his desk and forces him to acknowledge that she's more than just the nanny to him. Is he ready to risk his heart and build a new family?

YOU CAN FIND MORE INFORMATION ON UPCOMING HARLEQUIN TITLES, FREE EXCERPTS AND MORE AT HARLEQUIN.COM.

HSECNM0420

"Gracie, will you look at me?"

Stifling a sigh, she turned her head to face him. Those melty brown eyes were full of self-recrimination and regret.

"I'm sorry," he said. "I never should have touched you. I'm too old for you, and I'm not any kind of relationship material, anyway. I don't know what got into me, but I swear to you it's never going to happen again."

Hmm. How to respond?

Too bad there wasn't a large blunt object nearby. The guy deserved a hard bop on the head. What was wrong with him? No wonder it hadn't worked out with Marjorie. The man didn't have a clue.

But never mind. Gracie held it together as he apologized some more. She watched that beautiful mouth move and pondered the mystery of how such a great guy could have his head so far up his own ass.

Maybe if she yanked him close and kissed him, he'd get over himself and admit that last night had been amazing, the two of them had off-the-charts chemistry and he didn't want to walk away from all that goodness, after all.

Yeah, kissing him might shut him up and get him back on track for more hot sexy times. It had worked more than once already.

But come on. She couldn't go jumping on him and smashing her mouth on his every time he started beating himself up for having a good time with her.

No. A girl had to have a little pride.

He thought last night was a mistake?

Fair enough. She'd actually let herself believe for a minute or two there that they had something good going on, that her long dry spell manwise might be over.

But never mind about that. Let him have it his way. She would agree with him.

And then she would show him exactly what he was missing. And then, when he couldn't take it anymore and begged her for another chance, she would say that they couldn't, that he was too old for her and it wouldn't be right.

Don't miss
Their Secret Summer Family *by Christine Rimmer,*
available May 2020 wherever
Harlequin Special Edition books and ebooks are sold.

Harlequin.com

**Powerfully emotional, *New York Times*
bestselling author**

MAISEY YATES'S

**new novel is a heartwarming exploration of how
life's biggest challenges can turn into the greatest
opportunities of all...**

*Secrets from a
Happy Marriage*

"Fans of Robyn Carr and RaeAnne Thayne will enjoy
[Yates's] small-town romance." —*Booklist*

Order your copy today!

HQN

HQNBooks.com

Love Harlequin romance?

DISCOVER.

Be the first to find out about promotions,
news and exclusive content!

f Facebook.com/HarlequinBooks

y Twitter.com/HarlequinBooks

⊙ Instagram.com/HarlequinBooks

℗ Pinterest.com/HarlequinBooks

ReaderService.com

EXPLORE.

Sign up for the Harlequin e-newsletter and
download a free book from any series at
TryHarlequin.com

CONNECT.

Join our Harlequin community to
share your thoughts and connect
with other romance readers!
Facebook.com/groups/HarlequinConnection

HARLEQUIN

*Heartfelt or suspenseful,
inspiring or passionate, Harlequin
has your happily-ever-after.*

With new books published
every month, you are sure to find the
satisfying escape you know you deserve.